THE BOY IN BLUE DENIM

PATRICK E. CRAIG

COPYRIGHT

Cover by Cora Graphics Simona Cora Salardi

www.coragraphics.it

The Boy In Blue Denim

Copyright © 2023 by Patrick E. Craig

Published by P&J Publishing

P.O. Box 73

Huston, Idaho 83630

Library of Congress Cataloging-in-publications Data

Craig, Patrick E., 1947-

The Boy In Blue Denim / Patrick E. Craig

ISBN 979-8-9871451-3-5 (pbk.)

ISBN 9798987145128 (ebook)

CONTENTS

PRAISE FOR THE PORCH SWING MYSTERIES

THE BOY IN BLUE DENIM

Craig is able to skillfully combine the twists and turns of an Agatha Christie-Miss Marple murder mystery, and its suspense and edginess, with the rustic beauty of the Amish world and the aura of romance and peace that rests like a summer dew on its farms and homesteads. A page-turner not to be missed by fans of Amish fiction or fans of well-written murder mysteries both. A splendid effort by a seasoned author who excels at every genre he puts his hand to.

— Murray Pura CIBA, Word Guild, Selah Award-winning author

You could call it Amish fiction on steroids! The Boy in Blue Denim is a page-turner for sure. I have always liked the author's style and thoroughness of research, but this time he brought it to a new level. His characters are engaging and interesting. Their lives are intertwined in ways you would not expect. I read the book in two sittings because each page demanded I find out more. There are twists and turns you will not be expecting, and I suspect you won't want to put it down either!

— CONNIE PORTER

I read this book into the wee hours last night. It's amazing how the book hits on Newton's third law... For every action, there's a reaction and along the same lines... a ripple effect. One man's choice changed so many lives. His grief cause a line of grief...

I loved the story—so much suspense and so many surprises... Just when I thought I had the answer—boom! What the mind thought was truth turned out to be false. And yet I loved how all the pieces fell together in the end.

— JEAN MARIE

THE QUILT THAT KNEW

Patrick E. Craig has once again written a book that will take you deep into the heart of Amish country. *The Quilt That Knew* is a delightful and intriguing plain and simple mystery.

— VANNETTA CHAPMAN, USA TODAY BESTSELLING
AUTHOR

The Quilt That Knew is another great book by Patrick E. Craig. Jenny Hershberger and Bobby Halverson from the Apple Creek Dreams series are back, but now they are working on a cold murder case. This book had you sitting on the edge of your seat trying to figure out "who done it." Once I started reading it I could not put it down until I finished it. There were so many surprises and twists. First the dead girl in the box, then another dead body found in the woods, and finally the drug overdose of a main suspect. And when Jenny and Bobby start looking at these clues, mysterious things start to happen. This is a "must read" for everyone. I loved this book.

— KAY LEATHERS WINGO

So, how good is *The Quilt That Knew*? Well, I read it straight through in a day! And it's a great start to what will surely be a wonderful mystery series! And my favorite line:

"And I was thinking that the Amish community is not the peachy-keen, perfect world that most people think it is, especially those Englischers who buy those 'Amish fiction' books off the shelf at Walmart. Amish fiction, indeed!"

And, perhaps, my friends, that line best encapsulates what Patrick Craig does best—pure and honest portrayals of the Amish as people with real passions and faults, and not the idealistic fantasies of so many others. And that, is refreshing.

— SCOTT R. REZER — AUTHOR OF THE BUTCHER'S
BRIDE, THE LEPER KING AND LOVE ABIDETH STILL

A murder mystery set in an Amish community is surprising in itself; but a story that involves multiple murders? A popular cliche that we hear when discussing old houses is, *if those walls could talk.* In this tale by Patrick E. Craig, the investigators wish the quilt could talk. A retired sheriff and his Amish neighbor are called back to their old stomping grounds to assist in a 40 year old cold case that has been just recently uncovered. Jenny, with her knowledge of the Wooster, Ohio Amish community history finds that her mother's quilting journal is a key component to solving the crime. While trying to narrow the suspects, they encounter another related cold case and have to consider a current murder besides. Stitching all of this information together becomes quite the dilemma and following the action will keep you on pins and needles. Get yourself a copy of this yarn and try to piece it together for yourself.

— CALVIN DOUGLAS SMITH

DEDICATION

Dedicated to my wife, Judy, for her patience and understanding when she sees the the need to write come upon me...

ACKNOWLEDGEMENT

When I first started writing Amish fiction, I was blessed to be taken under the wing of Sicily Yoder, (Theresa Ann Phillips) an Amish author who grew up Amish and who opened the secrets of the Amish community to my researcher's mind. Any questions I asked her would be answered by pages of notes and information. Without her help I never would have gotten this far. Thank you Sicily.

A NOTE FROM PATRICK E. CRAIG

Imagine if Miss Marple was Amish—That's Jenny Hershberger solving her second murder mystery.

Many of you are very familiar with Jenny Hershberger. You met her in the Apple Creek Dreams series—*A Quilt For Jenna, The Road Home,* and *Jenny's Choice.*

Now Jenny is sixty-two and entering a new chapter in her life —as a detective. In the first book in **The Porch Swing Mysteries,** Jenny solved the mystery of **The Quilt That Knew,** the case of a missing girl found buried in a box in the woods forty years after her disappearance. Now Jenny is back in Book Two of The Porch Swing Mysteries, **The Boy In Blue Denim.**

She is living on her farm in Paradise, Pennsylvania. Old family friend Bobby Halverson, a retired sheriff, lives in a small cottage on the property. She is well known in her community since she wrote several books about the Amish, their history and customs. She also is the ghostwriter behind six Amish fiction novels. Everyone in town knows it, but nobody says much about it. She is Amish after all, and her elders try to look the other way.

But it is the column she writes for her local newspaper titled, "Dear Jenny," that draws her and Bobby into their second mystery. In response to an article in the paper about "The Boy In Blue Denim," an unidentified boy found murdered ten years before, Jenny receives a mysterious letter that points her toward a possible solution to the case. Jenny and Bobby team up once more with Detective Elbert Wainwright and return to Apple Creek to begin the investigation. As they dig deeper, they unearth secrets buried in secrets, and Jenny discovers things are not always as they seem.

One caveat. After you read this book, promise not to tell anybody how it ends.

Patrick E. Craig

1
———

THE SNOWS OF INDIANA

November, 1995

J ohnston Fairchild reached down to turn the heater knob on the dashboard of his tractor. It was all the way on. He drew the blanket closer around his legs.

Shoot. It is cold out here.

Outside the wrap-around window, the snow whirled in a frantic dance, propelled by the forty-mile-an-hour wind that blew the storm across two states from eastern Pennsylvania and landed it smack in the middle of Indiana. During the night, while he slept, the blizzard moved in like a freight train and caught Johnston with many of his cows still out in the storm. Now he was searching for the twenty head that he had not seen back at the feedlot.

Can't let one of them die, not at a dollar a pound for good beef cows.

The tractor sputtered, coughed, and then the engine died. The tractor rolled to a stop. Johnston stared at the dashboard.

What's going on?

The heater kept going, but the fan slowed way down. Johnston looked out the window. The snow was swirling, but the wind seemed to have died down... maybe. He turned off the key and there was silence—except for the howling of the wind that suddenly picked back up, and the creaks made by the ancient tractor frame as it shuddered in the gale.

Take it easy. You're close to the road. You can walk out.

Johnston buttoned up the top button of his parka and flipped the face flap over to cover his mouth. Then he opened the door of the cab. Instantly, the wind grabbed him and he felt the bitter chill through every layer of his clothes. He swung out, put his right foot down on the wheel, and found the step with his left. Then he was on the ground. He looked up at the tractor.

"Don't go anywhere. I'll be back in a while," he shouted. He grinned at his own joke and then looked around to get his bearings.

He had been traveling east along the fence that marked the forty acres at the bottom of his property. The fence was on his left-hand side. All he had to do was walk along it down to the east end of the pasture, climb the stile, and get out on the old farm track that ran along the section line that divided his land from Benjamin Stücker's place. Turn right, head south, and that would take him out to the lane and from there it was only a few hundred yards back to the house. He clapped his arms across his chest to warm himself, moved to the left about ten steps until he found the fence, and then started off.

The wind clutched at him with freezing fingers, pulling at his clothes as though to strip him naked and helpless in the monstrous cold.

Thank goodness Molly made me put on my long johns and thick wool socks. I can do this.

He trudged along, occasionally cussing the cold, his tractor, and the foot-deep snow. In about fifteen minutes, he came to the cross fence. He went to the right looking for the stile. Then he saw it, looming up out of the blinding white swirl of snow. Making his way through the two- and three-foot drifts that had piled against the fence, he grabbed the wooden rails and climbed over the fence. He was on the dirt track!

Across the road was Henry's Creek, lined by thick stands of cottonwood trees. Beyond the creek lay the woods that filled the back third of the Stücker farm. As a boy, he had played often in those woods and along the creek. There were many places to camp and deep holes in the creek where a kid could pull out crappie and perch or hunt crawdads with a piece of liver on a string.

He pushed on. The wind had died down and the morning light made it easier to see things around him. He recognized where he was.

Just here is where me and my brothers built ourselves a fort. Still there I bet.

On an impulse, he moved off the road and took a few steps toward the trees. There it was, still standing, although much the worse for years and wear. Old fence posts, scrounged two-by-fours, plywood, and some shingles left over from when his pop had re-roofed the farm house. Johnston saw the dark opening where the door used to hang and looked inside. He waited for a minute as his eyes adjusted to the dim light.

Yep. Pretty much like it was the last time I seen it. What, ten years ago?

He reached over to the shelf where they had kept their "stuff." Mad Magazines, candles, matches, Oreos, a couple of Zane Grey books. It was empty now, but back then it had been the real deal in kid forts. He sighed and turned to go. In the half-dark, he tripped on something and nearly fell. He caught himself on the doorjamb and banged his head on the wall.

"What the...?"

He looked down. Something lay by the wall. It was covered in a blanket or a tarp, he couldn't quite tell in the dim light.

Wait! It's the tarp we always left in here. What's under it?

He knelt and pulled the tarp back, then jerked away. Under the tarp was a body. It was a young boy, laid out on his back with his arms folded over his chest. He wore a blue shirt, dark overalls and a blue denim jacket, the kind any farm kid would have. He could see that the skin was blue.

Poor kid musta froze to death. I gotta get the sheriff!

Johnston Fairchild climbed out into the snow and went off down the road as fast as his legs could carry him.

———

THE FLASHING BLUE, YELLOW, AND RED LIGHTS MADE A kaleidoscope of patterns in the falling snow. Two sheriff's cars, an ambulance and three other emergency vehicles lined the dirt track in front of the old wooden structure. Sheriff Jimmy Clark stood outside, bundled up in his fur lined winter jacket with a Vermont ear-hat pulled down on his head instead of his usual Stetson. Inside the shack, he could see the flare of camera flashbulbs as the men from forensics took pictures of the body.

"Okay, Sheriff, we're done."

The two men came out and Jimmy stepped in. His sergeant followed with a large flashlight. The photographers had not disturbed the body, and it lay peacefully on its back. The dead person was a young boy, perhaps nine or ten. He wore a blue denim, long-sleeved shirt, dark denim overalls with the straps over the shoulders, and a blue denim jacket. His arms crossed over his chest, and his hair was slightly long, blond, recently and poorly cut. His face was regular and smooth, but he was quite thin. His eyes, a deep blue, were wide open. Laid out beside the boy were three items: A rainbow-colored stuffed horse, like you might win at a carnival, what appeared to be a child's reader, and a flat-brimmed Amish-style hat.

"Looks like he's Amish, Sheriff. Amish hat, clothes. What's the book?"

The sergeant put on his gloves and picked it up gently by the corner. It had a red cover and there was a picture of two young children putting coins into the cup held by a costumed monkey, while an old Italian organ grinder with white hair smiled at them.

"On Cherry Street—The Ginn Basic Reader. Looks like a book my mom had in school in the fifties. Where did that come from? And his eyes are open. He musta been awake when he died, Sheriff. Froze to death in the cold?"

Jimmy nodded. "Maybe... He's a good-looking kid, but how in the world did he get here?" The Sheriff knelt and looked closer. "And where did those bruises around his mouth come from?" Jimmy shook his head. "Ralph, get out an APB on any missing kids in the area. Get a picture in the local paper. He looks very Amish, so make sure you send some boys out to all the Amish farms. Bag all this stuff up. And call the coroner. I want a complete autopsy. Something is not right about this."

The Sergeant shook his head. "I don't know, Sheriff. Those folks are mighty close-mouthed when it comes to their own."

"I know, Ralph, but try anyway."

Sheriff Jimmy Clark stepped outside and nodded to the ambulance driver. "Okay, Sam, he's all yours."

Johnston Fairchild, who had been hanging around with the first responders, walked over. "Do you have any idea who the kid is, Sheriff? I've never seen him in town. And how did he wind up in my old fort?"

Jimmy shook his head again. "I don't have the foggiest, Johnston. I've never seen him either. He looks Amish, though, so if he lived around here, he wouldn't have spent much time in town. We'll check with the Amish, see if we can find out anything."

Johnston frowned. "Good luck with that, Sheriff."

THE NEXT DAY, JIMMY GOT A CALL FROM GEORGE FRANKLIN, THE county coroner.

"Hey, George, what do you have for me?"

"Well, Jimmy, I'm not sure yet, but I don't think the kid froze to death."

"No?"

"Nope, I'm pretty sure he froze after he died. When I got him undressed and turned him over, I observed livor mortis."

"Livor mortis? What's that? I've heard of rigor mortis…"

"Livor mortis usually begins thirty minutes to four hours after death and is most pronounced twelve hours after death. Because the heart has stopped beating, gravity pulls the blood down, resulting in the pooling of blood at the lowest point in the body. It was five degrees above zero the night of the storm, so the body froze quickly. That stopped the process, but the boy had been dead long enough before he froze for me to see a slight pooling all along his back and the back of his legs."

"Well, what killed him then?"

"I can't say for sure, but I would guess suffocation. Somebody held something over his nose and mouth and he suffocated."

Sheriff Clark was intrigued now. "How can you tell?"

"His eyes, Sheriff. They were very bloodshot. When you cut off someone's oxygen, the tiny vessels in the eyes burst and the eyes become very bloodshot. And there are bruises around the mouth. So, my take is someone killed him, laid him out, and left him there. He was thin but not emaciated and there was an old bruise on his right buttock, like someone hit him once with a strap. Regular kid stuff, I guess."

"Boy, George, that throws a whole new light on this. Well, somebody must know who he is. We'll keep looking. And thanks."

Three weeks later, Jimmy was sitting at his desk. There was a knock on the door.

"Come!"

Sergeant Ralph Hastings came in with a sheaf of papers in his hand.

"Well?"

Ralph shook his head. "Nada, zip, *nichts,* as the Amish would say. We covered every farm for fifty miles around. No one's ever seen this kid. It's as though he dropped out of the sky."

Jimmy spread the local paper out on the desk.

"This has been running every day for three weeks. Every day it moves further toward the back of the paper. They called him, 'The Boy In Blue Denim.'"

On the page were two pictures of the boy, one closeup of the face and the other a full-length body shot. "No calls, no letters, nothing. You're right. It's as though he fell out of a plane or something."

"I got a call from George, Sheriff. We are going to have to get the kid in the ground. It's been three weeks. George is a good undertaker, but he's not that good."

Jimmy nodded. "I know. I was just hoping for a lead, someone who knew him, anybody, just a little clue." He sighed and closed the paper. "Okay, Ralph, set it up with George. I'll see if I can get the state to pay for a box. And we'll need a headstone. Don't want to just put him in the ground."

Two days later, the sheriff, his sergeant, the coroner, and the sheriff's wife stood by an open grave in the local cemetery. A man in a black suit stood at the head of the grave, the local Presbyterian Pastor. Several yards off, the grave attendants stood with the owner of the cemetery. The simple pine box, purchased from a local Amish woodworker, was nothing remarkable, just pine. The lowering straps were in place.

"Okay, Jerry." The Sheriff looked at the pastor.

The pastor opened his Bible. "Lord, we did not know this boy. We do not know where he came from or what his life was like. But you do. You know all things. Oh, we know some things. This boy's earthly struggle is at an end. We also know the God we worship is a God of grace and mercy and you will do right by each person. We hope that this boy had not attained the age of accountability and was still an innocent in your eyes. We ask that you will receive this young person into your arms in the hope of the glorious resurrection purchased by our Lord on Calvary's cross. We do not presume to know his eternal destiny, but we know this..."

The pastor opened his Bible and read.

But we do not want you to be uninformed, brothers, about those who are asleep, that you may not grieve as others do who have no hope. For since we believe that Jesus died and rose again, even so, through Jesus, God will bring with him those who have fallen asleep. For this we declare to you by a word from the Lord, that we who are alive, who are left until the coming of the Lord, will not precede those who have fallen asleep. For the Lord himself will descend from heaven with a cry of command, with the voice of an archangel, and with the sound of the trumpet of God. And the dead in Christ will rise first. Then we who are alive, who are left, will be caught up together with them in the clouds to meet the Lord in the air, and so we will always be with the Lord. Therefore, encourage one another with these words. I Thessalonians 4:13-18.

"Amen."

The rest of the group said amen and then turned to go. Sheriff Jimmy turned to the owner of the cemetery. "Did you get the headstone?"

"Yes, Sheriff. Just like you said." He held it up. Small, nothing really.

Jimmy looked at the stone. Inscribed on it were seven simple words.

"Johnny Doe—The Boy In Blue Denim."

A VERY COLD CASE

April, 2005

Detective Elbert Wainwright put down the Sudoku he was working on and sighed. Outside it was drizzling a light rain, April showers, and everything was on hold. Life in Wayne County for the last month had been tame, very tame indeed. No robberies, no major car crashes, no domestic violence, not even a DUI. It was as though everyone in his part of Ohio was on best behavior, and it was driving him nuts.

"What good is it being a detective if there is nothing to detect?" he said to the vase of flowers his secretary always put on his desk. He put his finger on the intercom button, intending to ask Janice if there was anything happening out there, but he realized the question might sound somewhat awkward. After all, he was the lead detective of the Wooster police force and he, of all people, should be the one with his finger on the pulse of the town.

He got up and walked to the window. The drizzle had picked up and was now a steady downpour.

I guess this is what they call cabin fever.

Then he had a thought. He went back to the desk and thumbed the intercom button.

"Yes, Detective?"

"Janice, how big is the cold case file?"

"Um, let me look. I'll be right back."

Elbert waited. He picked up a pencil and drummed out a beat from one of the nameless tunes he heard on AM radio on his way to work. Bump bump tap..., bump bump tap..., bump bump...

The intercom clicked. "Forty."

"Forty?"

"Yes, Detective, forty unsolved cases. Fifteen local and twenty-five in the tri-state area outside Wayne County."

"Can you bring me the files?"

"That bored, huh, Detective?"

Two hours later, Elbert was on his fifteenth read. All of them had been routine local cases. A missing husband—missing from a wife who used to hit him with a frying pan—a no-brainer. There was a lost champion bulldog worth $20,000, another no-brainer. A very special package missing off the front porch of a house in Wooster—at least it had been special to the old woman who didn't get her birthday present. The local stuff had been a series of lost causes and very petty, so he expanded his horizons and started checking cases in the tri-state area—Ohio, Indiana, and Kentucky. It was when he opened the twenty-first case that he stopped and took another look.

A young boy stared up at him. He was lying on what looked like a tarp. Longish blonde hair, roughly cut, regular features, blue eyes, and dressed in denim—a denim shirt, coat, and overalls. His arms were folded over his chest, and there was light bruising around his mouth. Elbert looked for a long time—something about the kid really resonated, drew him in. He turned to the next page. Now it was a closeup of the boy's face. The eyes were fixed, staring at something beyond him, or so it seemed.

The boy intrigued him.

He looks Amish. What's his story?

He read through the case history. Young boy, nine or ten years old, dressed in denim clothes, found smothered to death in the woods of Indiana. There were pictures of the funeral and his headstone.

Johnny Doe—The Boy In Blue Denim.

There were also pictures of the strange items found with the boy—a flat-brimmed Amish style hat, a very old first grade reader, and a rainbow-colored stuffed toy horse.

Who is this kid? Why the book and the horse? Something about this case...

A thought crossed his mind and his finger went to the intercom buzzer.

"Yes?"

"Janice, can you get me Jack Simpson over at the Daily Record?"

"Sure."

A few minutes later, the intercom buzzed. "Jack Simpson on line 2."

Elbert picked up the phone and punched the keypad. "Jack?"

"Good afternoon, Detective. What can I do for you?"

"Well... I've been going through cold cases here at the office and..."

"That bored, huh?"

Elbert laughed. "Yeah, that bored. Same question Janice asked. Jack, I've stumbled onto something that really piques my interest and I thought you might help me out."

"Well, Elbert, I owe you a couple. Haven't forgotten about the scoop you sent me on that corruption case up at the state capitol. What can I do for you?"

"I found an unsolved case involving a young boy who the authorities think was murdered ten years ago out in Indiana, forty miles across the state line from Ohio."

"Think was murdered?"

"Yeah. The day the boy died, there was a big storm in the area and the temperatures were way below freezing. When they found the body, the police figured the kid had gotten lost in the storm and frozen to death. But the coroner in LaGrange County thinks the kid suffocated first. He's ninety percent sure the kid was dead before the body froze."

"Anything else?"

"By his clothes in the pictures, I would say he is Amish. He was laid out like he was in a viewing and there were some interesting items set out beside him."

"Like what, Elbert?"

"A flat Amish hat, a first-grade primer from the nineteen fifties, and a rainbow-colored toy horse, like something you might win at a carnival."

"That's a very eclectic mix of items, Elbert. So how can I help?"

"Can you run a picture of the kid with an article? You know, like a cold case revisited deal? Just on the off chance that something might turn up?"

"Tell you what, Elbert. I could do a story on some of the more mysterious cold cases in the tri-state area and feature The Boy In Blue Denim. It's a catchy name, anyway."

"Jack, that would be great. And can you hit the Amish angle? That might inspire some of our recalcitrant Amish neighbors to come forward... if they have any information. We might learn something new."

"I'll get right on it, Elbert. Sounds like an interesting story. Can you send over a picture?"

"Sure thing, Jack. I'll messenger it over today."

"Good. I'll let you know when the story is going to run."

———

At the end of that week, Elbert got a call from Jack Simpson.

"Hey, Jack! What's up?"

"Elbert, just wanted to let you know I put that article together. We are running it in the Sunday edition."

"That's great, Jack."

"Well, there's more."

"What's that?"

"Our syndicator rep dropped by this week and asked me if I was writing anything interesting. I told him about The Boy In Blue Denim and he wants to pick it up."

"What does that mean, Jack?"

"What it means, Detective, is your story is going out to one hundred papers from Indiana to Pennsylvania. Readership should be several hundred thousand."

———

Elbert had several papers spread out on his desk. They all had The Boy In Blue Denim as a feature. One from Wooster, Jack's paper, but then there was one from Cincinnati, Columbus and Akron, Ohio; Fort Wayne and Indianapolis, Indiana; Chicago, Illinois; Pittsburg and Philadelphia, Pennsylvania; and several more from the Amish areas of Ohio, Pennsylvania, and Indiana.

There he was, Johnny Doe—The Boy In Blue Denim, staring out at the world. Elbert shook his head.

Who would kill a kid and then lay him out like a funeral viewing? A nut job or a dope head, probably... or somebody who cared about him.

Elbert noticed Jack had given the Wooster police station hotline for tips and responses. He pushed the button on the intercom.

"Yes, Detective?"

"Any responses to this article yet?"

"Hmmm, let me see... Oh, about five hundred. In fact, the hotline department is a little ticked with us. They called and said they wished you would have at least given them a heads-up."

"Five hundred? Wow! How do I listen to them?"

"Well, they make a recording of all the calls, so I imagine you can get a CD and play it on your computer."

"Okay, will you have them send that over?"

"You going to listen to all of them?"

"I might."

FOUR HOURS LATER, ELBERT WISHED HE HAD KEPT HIS FINGER OFF the button and his mouth shut. He had listened to at least twenty theories about reptile aliens killing the boy, thirty more about the CIA's involvement, a bunch where people blamed the local drunk or hophead in an effort to clean up their town, and at least five putting forth the theory nobody knew who the boy was because he was actually a girl disguised as a boy, and if they only looked for missing girls from that year their case would be solved in a New York minute.

One caller believed that the crime had something to do with a foster home located several miles from the scene of the crime. A woman from West Virginia, after first confessing on the tip line, went to the local police station and confessed to the murder. The fact she was securely locked in a mental institution at the time of the crime didn't help her confession.

Several callers insisted that the dead boy was a young man

who someone kidnapped outside a supermarket in Philadelphia. They conveniently overlooked the year of the kidnapping: 1955.

And so went the afternoon. There were a few tips that seemed promising, but most were dead ends at best and bizarre at worst.

One that he took a longer look at was the case of a family who traveled with carnivals. The caller reminded the hot line that the family had a daughter who died from neglect and malnutrition. Instead of burying their young daughter in a cemetery, the parents wrapped their daughter in a blanket and left her body in a wooded area in southern Ohio. The police investigated the family and discovered that several of their children had starved to death and none of them received a proper burial. Elbert dug out the case but wrote it off after he decided that the boy's murder did not fit any of the facts.

<hr>

After a very frustrating afternoon, Elbert called it a day. He was packing up to go home when the intercom buzzed.

"Make it quick, Janice. I'm headed home."

"Detective, there is a call for you that you probably want to take."

"Who is it?"

"Jenny Hershberger."

3

JENNY GETS A LETTER

J enny Hershberger peeked in the door at Gary Phillips, editor at the Paradise Post, the local paper in her town of Paradise, Pennsylvania. Gary looked up and smiled.

"Jenny! Now my week is off to a great start."

Jenny grinned. It was Monday morning, the day she always stopped by to pick up any letters readers had sent in to "Ask Jenny," her column on all things Amish. She'd been writing it for twenty-five years now and Gary had been the editor the whole time.

"Did I get any letters?"

Gary nodded and pointed to a stack of letters on his desk. "Only one hundred and twelve this week." He laughed. "The conference room is open, and the coffee is hot. Make yourself at home. Did you bring Undie?"

They both laughed. Undie was Jenny's name for her old Underwood typewriter, the one her papa had given her so many years before. As antiquated as the machine was, it still worked well and with care and attention and a yearly trip to a local man who still repaired them for fun, Undie had stayed workable.

"Yes, Gary. I brought Undie."

Jenny picked up the pile, grabbed up the case that was Undie's home away from home, and made her way down the hall. She stopped at the coffee station and poured herself a cup, marling it with cream from the pitcher beside the pot. Then, balancing her coffee while holding on to the rest of her stuff, she went into the conference room and sat down. She spread the letters out on the table, picked one at random, and opened it.

Dear Jenny,

I'm a new reader and I don't know too much about the Amish. My husband is in the military. He's stationed at the Marine Reserve Center in Enola. We're from California, so I've never seen any Amish people until I came here. I have been reading your column for about five months and have learned a lot, but I still have some questions. Number one—do the Amish have hot water if they don't use electricity? Are they allowed to use propane or natural gas? Number two—Do the Amish ever use a telephone? I know these are silly questions, so you can send me a note if you don't want to answer me in the paper.

Greta

Jenny read the letter again. Many people over the years asked similar questions. It had been a while since she did an article on the Amish and their separation from the technological world, so she decided this would be a good time for another. She opened the case, took out her typewriter, rolled in a sheet of paper, and began.

Dear Greta,

I so appreciate your letter. It is not silly at all. There are always many people who are new to the ways of the Amish, so your letter has prompted me to write this article. First, I will start with the Amish themselves and their relationship to and with modern technology.

As you have discovered, there is a group of traditionalist people, who reject much of modern society's technology, including electricity from the public grid. They are the Amish. Back in the days before America was 'wired up' with an electrical grid, it was easier for the Amish to stay 'disconnected' since there was nothing to connect to. But with the coming of modernization, the Amish had to make some adjustments.

The power itself is not the issue. Running household items with electricity, like an iron or a lamp, is perfectly harmonious with Amish belief and tradition. The Amish welcome technology that adds value to the Amish community, although each community decides for itself just what is valuable to them.

You may not know this, but there are many Amish affiliations and like the Jewish faith, which enfolds everything from strict Orthodox Jews to very liberal reformed Jews, the Amish vary in the application of their use of technology. There are Amish who would never drive a car but will accept a ride in one. There are also Amish who own and drive cars. There are Amish who will not own a phone but will build a local center with phones in it for community use, while there are many Amish who use personal phones to conduct their daily business. There are Amish who would use nothing but horse or mule-drawn equipment to harvest their crops, but if you go to Shipshewana, Indiana, in the summer, the Amish have a wonderful display of old gas-powered tractors and steam driven harvest equipment at their annual fair.

So, it is not the technology itself, but the connection to the power grid or the telephone grid that is troubling. The Amish want to remain separate from the non-Amish world as much as they can. They fear that being too close to the 'Englisch,' (as they call all non-Amish), would unduly influence their culture. Back in 1920, the Amish saw that electricity does not discriminate, and eliminating public power from the home eliminates the temptation to use television, radio, or now, in more modern times, the internet. Also, the Amish feel that too much dependence on labor-saving devices deprives children of character-building opportunities to work hard.

So, in answer to your question, even though the Amish mostly refuse to buy power from the public grid, they still depend on energy for their everyday operations. The Amish are practical people and have come up with many ingenious workarounds. To power appliances, they use batteries, propane gas, compressed air, various generators, hydraulic pumps, and even solar panels. However, they do not connect to the natural gas lines that so many cities provide or the transformers that sit on the poles near their homes. Many people think of the Amish as backward, but there is a vast difference between backward and separate. The Amish often use electric lights instead of candles or oil lamps. They have solar-powered electric fences, propane powered refrigerators and washers, electric tools and, back in 2008, someone even developed a Classic Word Processor, also known as the 'Amish Computer.' The designer developed it specifically for the plain people, and it comes without connectivity ports, sound, pictures, games, or other features beyond the ability to process documents and be useful for business.

I must confess, I thought about buying one, but I am too fond of my old Underwood typewriter, which was a present to me from my papa when I first became a writer. But that's another story.

I hope this is helpful.

Jenny.

Jenny smiled and set the article aside. Writing about the Amish had always been a source of great joy for her. It was the historian in her that longed to dig and dig into the history and ways of people, especially her people. She remembered sitting at her mama's feet trying to learn to make quilts and quickly understanding that for her, making a quilt would be as easy as flying from Apple Creek to New York using her arms for power. Hopeless.

She always thanked *du lieber Gott* for parents that could see what the Lord was doing in her life long before she did. Her mama knew her adopted daughter would never be a master quilter like she was, but they both knew their daughter and could see how *Gott* was shaping Jenny. They allowed her to become an intern at the Wooster Public Library, even after her 'official' time of schooling ended in the eighth grade. It was there she discovered history and the BGMI, The Birth and Genealogy Master Index, an exhaustive record of most of the families in the United States and their origins. It was through this book she had started her studies on her own family and with it and other sources, traced the Springers and the Hershbergers back to Switzerland and even beyond to Princess Isabella of Poland, the woman who was the Matriarch of the Hershberger family and whom Jenny came to know as The Mennonite Queen.

Her studies also helped her lead the man who became her husband back to his own Amish roots.

Weren't those wonderful days? When Jonathan and I sat in the library together for hours and he discovered why the Amish life always drew him.

She sighed and picked up the next letter. It followed pretty much on the same lines as the first, and in fact most of them did. There were several asking for recipes, which she often used as a filler, and requesting the names and addresses of different Amish businesses.

Then she came to a letter that stopped her in her tracks.

Dear Jenny,

A few days ago, your paper ran an article about what I guess the police call cold cases—cases that have been around for a long time and never solved. One case, called "The Boy In Blue Denim," really got my attention. There was a picture of a small boy the police found deceased ten years ago in a snowstorm in Indiana. Well, I swear I saw a picture of that boy about ten years ago. I was at the Quilt Fair in Dalton, Ohio...

Jenny jerked as though someone had slapped her.

The Quilt Fair in Dalton! My mama was going to that fair back in 1950 when she got caught in the huge snowstorm, the snowstorm that I was lost in, too. Somehow, Mama found me and saved me. And now here's a letter about a boy lost in a snowstorm...

She read on.

...where I met an Amish lady from Shipshewana who was showing her quilts at the Fair. We struck up a conversation, and she began brag-ging about her grandson. She reached in her purse and got out a picture of her one grandson, a very recent one. Jenny, I know the picture she

showed me was the boy in the newspaper article in your paper—the one they call The Boy In Blue Denim. He was a lovely child, and that's why I remembered. So handsome—blond, blue eyes, his little Amish hat.

The woman, Amanda, was very shy because, as you know, the Amish are not big on taking pictures. But she was so proud of him. Anyway, the article said that if you have any information about this boy, please contact the police. Well, I'm a little reticent about getting involved personally, so I thought I would contact you.

I heard how you solved the mystery of that girl buried in the box, so I thought to myself, this is right up Jenny's alley. It may not lead anywhere, but I'll give you what I have. Like I said, she's an Amish quilter from Shipshewana, Indiana. That's not a lot to go on, but it's worth checking out.

Roberta Kelley

Jenny got up, went out, and walked down the hall to Gary's office and knocked

"Come."

She went in with the letter in her hand.

"What, got a good one?"

Jenny shook her head. "I don't know, Gary. First, did you run an article about cold cases a few days ago?"

"Sure did. It came in through our syndicator. A detective out in Ohio is looking for help with some old cases."

"Was part of the story about a boy wearing denim?"

"Yep. The Boy In Blue Denim. He was the headliner. Let me look."

Gary got up and walked to a long table under his window. There were piles of the paper stacked there. He rummaged through and pulled out a copy. He spread it out on his desk and flipped through the pages until he found what he was looking for.

"Here he is."

Jenny went over and looked down. A face looked up at her—a small boy, maybe eight to ten years old, blonde hair, dressed in typical Amish denim. He was lying on what looked like a tarp and next to him was an Amish style straw hat, a book, and a toy horse. She caught her breath. His eyes were open, and he seemed to look right into her soul.

"Where was he found?"

"In Indiana somewhere. It says that at first, they thought he had frozen to death, but then the coroner investigated and concluded that someone suffocated him first. So, it's a murder case. I guess some detective in Ohio was going through cases and this one caught his eye."

Jenny nodded. "I can see why."

"What's this all about, Jenny?"

"I got a letter from a woman today who says she met this boy's grandmother at the Dalton Quilt Fair over ten years ago. The grandmother showed her a picture of this boy. I won't go into why that fair and the unusual circumstances of his death are so relevant to me, but they are."

"Did she give you a name?"

"Yes. It seems the grandmother is from Shipshewana, her name is Amanda, and she's Amish. That's all she had."

She looked down at the newspaper. "Did the article include the name of the detective?"

"Sure did. It says if you have any information, contact him."

"What's his name?"

Gary looked. "Ah, here it is." He looked up. "Elbert Wainwright, Wooster Police Department."

Jenny shook her head and chuckled.

"What?"

"Of course, it's Elbert. I know him. He and I and Bobby Halverson worked on a case together last year in Apple Creek, my home town."

Gary smiled. "The girl in the box."

"Yes, that's the one. Very interesting that he's involved in all this."

She looked down at the boy again. Something wrenched at her heart.

I'm sorry, little boy. I'm sorry nobody came to save you like my mama saved me...

Jenny felt a tear start down her cheek.

I'll do what I can for you, I promise.

4

GOING HOME AGAIN

The intercom on Detective Elbert Wainwright's desk buzzed. He pressed the button.

"Yes, Janice?"

"Call for you, Detective."

"Name?"

"Jenny Hershberger. Line one."

Elbert pressed the button. "Jenny Hershberger! How are you?"

"Hello Detective Wainwright."

"Jenny, I thought we were past titles."

"Yes, we are, Elbert, but since this is an official call..."

"Official?"

"Yes. I'm calling in response to the Boy In Blue Denim story that you sent out."

Elbert nodded to himself.

Of course, you are.

"Really? What about it?"

"I have some information that may be of value to you."

"Shoot."

"Well... a woman in our area saw the article in the local paper. I guess the Paradise Post gets syndicated material that they use to fill out the empty spaces in what is otherwise lots of discussion about the weather, crops, recipes, gardening tips, Little League games and the American Legion barbecue."

Elbert smiled. "They do the same here."

"Well, this woman, Roberta Kelley, is not Amish, but she has a genuine interest in the Amish, so she visits a lot of the quilting fairs and exhibitions, and antique shops."

"I have an aunt like that. Go on."

"Roberta saw your story and recognized the little boy. At least she claims she did."

Elbert sat up in his chair. "How sure was she?"

"Very sure, Elbert. And here's the strange part. A little over ten years ago, she was in Dalton, at the big quilt fair. She met a woman who was displaying her quilts, and they got into a conversation. The woman showed Roberta a picture of her grandson. It struck Roberta how handsome the young boy was, and that's why she remembered him when she saw your picture."

Elbert picked up a pencil. "What's the strange part?"

"In 1950, my mother, my adoptive mother, Jerusha Springer, was on her way to the Dalton Quilt Fair when she got lost in a huge snowstorm."

"Yes?"

"I was also lost in that storm. A man kidnapped me in Pennsylvania, and when he was driving west in the storm, he went off the road and slid his car onto Jepson's Pond, right outside of Dalton. He got out of the car, leaving me in the back seat, and fell through the ice and drowned. I was alone and slowly freezing to death in the car. Mama found me when she was trying to get to Jepson's cabin to get out of the storm..."

There was a pause.

"Jenny?"

"Forgive me, Elbert. I am getting very emotional about this."

Elbert heard Jenny take a deep breath, and then she went on.

"My editor gave me the article and when I read the details, I realized the little boy had died in a snowstorm. The connection to that and the Dalton Fair stirred something in my heart. It troubled me... that Mama saved me from a tremendous storm, but no one saved this poor boy. I'm not sure what the Lord is doing, but I want to help. I feel very connected to this little boy. And then when I saw you are the detective that is pursuing the investigation, I just knew I had to call."

"Did this Roberta get the grandmother's name?"

"Just her first name—Amanda. But the woman is an Amish quilter, and she lives in Shipshewana. We might find her if we go to the Amish elders."

Elbert shook his head.

This is strange, and that's for sure.

Elbert thought for a moment and then spoke. "Sooo, Jenny…"

"Yes, Elbert?"

"Do you think you could come out and do some field work for me?"

There was a momentary silence. "May I bring Bobby?"

Elbert smiled.

Great minds think alike.

"I was going to suggest that. Same deal as last time. You will work for my department and I'll get you a remuneration and expenses. As a retired police officer, Bobby can be the official liaison to my department. And I'll FedEx copies of the case files so you can go over what I've got so far."

Elbert tapped his pencil on the desk. "This may lead to something, Jenny, or it might not. But I'm under my budget for the year, so I can afford to mess around with this case a little. I feel very connected to this boy as well."

Another pause. "Send your information then, and I'll talk to Bobby and let you know. Goodbye, Elbert."

"Goodbye, Jenny."

Bobby Halverson cupped his hands around the warm mug of coffee. He had been walking down the hill from his cottage with his dog, Rufus, when Jenny called him from her porch. It was a very chill November day in Pennsylvania, overcast and threatening snow. He had forgotten his gloves and appreciated the hot beverage Jenny poured for him. Rufus, in the meantime, curled up in front of Jenny's fire and promptly went to sleep.

"Elbert wants us to come out, eh?"

Jenny took a sip. "Yes, there is at least one trip to be made concerning the case and I think, since he is tied to his office, he appreciates that we can be more mobile."

"Trip to where?"

"Shipshewana for sure, and maybe others, if that is not a dead end."

"That's quite a ways from Wooster." Bobby took another sip. "Well, if we go, he'll have to get us a car. My old truck is good for driving down the hill to get my mail and running into town, but that's about it. Those rocker arms are just about gone."

Bobby put down his cup. "Can you give me some background on this case?"

Jenny got up and left, and when she returned, she had an open FedEx envelope in her hand with several sheets visible. She pulled some pictures from the envelope. Bobby looked them over. A small boy, dressed Amish style, blond, blue eyes.

"Elbert overnighted this to me and I've gone through it. Ten years ago, a farmer looking for some stray cows in a snowstorm stumbled across this young boy dead in an abandoned shed off an old farm lane that separates his property from a neighbor's. The boy, as you can see, wore Amish-style clothing—blue denim overalls, a blue shirt, and a denim jacket... plus his Amish hat was with him. He appeared to have frozen to death, but after an examination, the Coroner was ninety-nine percent sure that someone smothered him before he froze."

"Where did they find him?"

"Just across the Ohio State line in northern Indiana."

"What are those other things with him?"

"A first-grade reader from the fifties and a toy horse."

"There's a diverse collection."

Jenny nodded. "Yes, but if this Amanda is his grandmother, they may help in making a positive identification."

"Very true... So, what's the plan? And why are you so interested in this case?"

"Bobby, remember where we met?"

Bobby smiled. "In the heart of the worst snowstorm in Ohio history, that's where. Your mama wrapped you in the Rose of Sharon quilt in Jepson's cabin to keep you from freezing. Your papa and I drove my old tractor through twenty-foot drifts to find you."

"And where was my mama going when she got lost in that storm?"

"To the Dalton Quilt..." Bobby stopped and his eyes opened a bit. "Oh. I am seeing the connection."

"Yes, and I felt that connection when I looked into that little boy's eyes in the picture. He was lost in a snowstorm, Bobby, but no one saved him. I feel like he's been lost ever since then. I know he has a name, a mother, a father. And I want to help him. I want him to be with his people. And if we can, I want to find out who killed him, and bring them to justice."

"Sounds like something we should do, Jenny. Where do we start?"

"I need to call my cousin Jared and see if my old house is still empty. If it is, we can probably use it as our headquarters again. We will need to get a car and have some meetings with Elbert and see what comes from that. I also need to let Rachel and Daniel know we will be gone so they can keep an eye on the place..."

Bobby reached for a Camel in his shirt pocket and, remembering where he was, stopped. "...and make sure they feed Rufus."

"When are you going to give those cigarettes up, Uncle Bobby?"

He shrugged his shoulders. "Jenny, I'm eighty-two years old. I'm in pretty good shape for my age except for this Amish-food doughnut around my middle. The doc says my lungs are in great shape. I have cut back to three a day, but you know, some things are hard to let go of."

"That's for sure."

Bobby pulled the packet over. "Can I look through this stuff?"

"Go ahead. And while you are here, you might as well have some breakfast casserole and help me finish that pot of *kaffee*."

Bobby put his arm behind his back, pushed it up, and grimaced. "Okay, okay, you twisted my arm. I'll stay for breakfast."

***

LATER THAT DAY, JENNY GOT IN TOUCH WITH HENRY LOWENSTEIN, her friend and next-door neighbor from childhood in Apple Creek. Being an *Englischer,* Henry had a phone at his house and Jenny had the number.

"Jenny! So good to hear your voice. Are you coming home?"

Home!

Jenny got a catch in her voice. "Well... um... that depends on some things falling into place first."

"How can I help?"

"Well, I need to find out if my house is still empty. Last time we were there, Jared moved up to the big house, and we stayed in the old place."

"The house is empty, Jenny. I think Jared hopes that someday you will move back here. He and his wife have kept it just like Jerusha and Reuben kept it. Nothing has changed."

"Is the swing still on the front porch?"

"Sure is. Just waiting for you to come on home and do some swinging… Jenny?"

Jenny's throat constricted. So many memories. So many difficult times worked through, out in the porch swing.

"Jenny?"

"… Yes… Henry. Excuse me…. um… Can you have Jared call me? Bobby and I are coming back to Apple Creek to help Detective Wainwright on another case, and we would love to stay at… at home."

"Well, isn't that fine! And don't you know I was just talking to Jared last week, and he said he hoped you would come again sometime. The old place seemed to come to life the last time you were here. Like when your mama and papa were alive…" Henry coughed and took a breath.

"For sure and certain Jenny, I miss the Springer family living next door. Your papa was awful good to me. And yes, I'll have Jared call you. What's the number?"

"I'm going to give you Bobby's number. It's 717-442-8765. He lives on my place in Paradise and he can give me the message. Just ask Jared if it's okay if we come."

"Okay, Jenny. Will do. It will be good to see you again."

"And you, Henry. Good bye."

5

GETTING STARTED

J enny was busy in her bedroom at the farmhouse in Paradise. Henry had called Bobby. Her cousin Jared had confirmed the use of the Springer house as their headquarters in Apple Creek, so Bobby contacted Elbert and let him know they were coming. Now she was putting together her clothes for the trip. As she looked through her drawers, she came upon a faded envelope under her clothes in the bottom drawer.

What's this?

She opened it and took out the contents. It was a picture she and her husband, Jonathan, had taken together at a roadside amusement park when they were running away together, over forty years before.

She sat down on the bed.

Oh, my goodness! I forgot all about this picture.

A flood of memories came pouring into her heart. The picture was from one of those 'take your own Polaroid' stands where you cram into a narrow booth and get three poses for a dollar. It was in the days before Jonathan had joined the Amish church. His hair was still long, tied back in a ponytail. She had cut her hair and was not wearing a *kappe*. The red curls made her look like Shirley Temple. She chuckled.

What was I thinking?

They both looked very *Englisch*. There were two silly poses where they were sticking their tongues out, and one serious— their faces touching as they looked into each other's eyes.

We were so young, and foolish, and so desperately in love...

Jonathan's face swam before her eyes. She reached for the hanky in her pocket.

That was forty-four years ago. You were so handsome and so confused... but I saw something in you. You were lost, like the little boy in blue denim, and it seemed like you couldn't find your way home. But then Gott stepped in...

Jenny got up and went to the dresser. Made of clear pine, it was the first big project that Jonathan had undertaken after Grandfather Borntraeger taught him woodworking. The detailing was coarse and the lines of the piece awkward, but she had loved it from the moment Jonathan moved it into their room. She remembered him standing proudly beside it as she ran her hands over the top and opened each drawer as though it were a treasure trove.

She loved the smell of the linseed oil that he rubbed into the wood and when she spread a lace piece over the top and placed her things there, it had become a symbol of all that Jonathan had left behind from his old hippie life, and all that he had become to be with her. Now she picked up one object on the top of the dresser, a small box. A sharp, almost physical pain touched her heart as she opened the lid. Inside were several folded pieces of paper. She took one out, slowly spread it open on the dresser, and read. She traced her fingers over Jonathan's cursive, firm on the paper.

My precious Jenny,

It is the end of another long day here in Paradise. I have been in the fields since daybreak with Grandfather Borntraeger. As soon as the thaw came and the soil warmed, we began preparing the ground for spring planting. This is the hardest work I've ever done; yet it is the most fulfilling. Your grandfather is a kind man, but he is very strict and does not put up with any complaining or questioning of his methods. Since I am so new to this, he must teach me as we work. I feel like a little boy all over again, but he is very patient with me, even when I make mistakes.

Jenny folded the letter and placed it back in the box. Tears formed in her eyes and rolled silently down her cheeks. She stood silently by the dresser and stared at her reflection in the mirror. Now the red curls were gone, replaced by silver, still rambunctious though and taking every chance to peek mischievously out from under her *kappe.*

It's as though you are trying to tell me something, Jonathan.

There was a knock at the door, then a voice. "Mama? You here?"

Rachel...

Her daughter Rachel came into the room. "What are you doing, Mama?"

"Packing."

Rachel's eyebrows arched. "And just where do you think you are going?"

"Well, I was going to tell you, but it has just happened in a rush. Your Uncle Bobby and I are going back to Apple Creek to help Elbert... Detective Wainwright, with a case."

"Another case? Wasn't the last one exciting enough for you?"

"Well... it was very interesting."

Rachel stared at her mother with that 'Well?' look on her face. "Well?"

Jenny laughed. "I knew that was coming. Well... what?"

"Well, aren't you going to tell me about it?"

"Only if you make a pot of *kaffee* and we can sit for a while. I've been packing all morning."

"Done."

kaffee, they had indulged in some date pudding cobbler that Jenny had learned to make from a recipe sent in by a reader.

Rachel finished her cup. "That's a very interesting case, Mama. And you say that you got a letter from a lady who knew who the boy was?"

"Yes, and she gave me the first name of the grandmother... who she met at the Dalton Quilt Fair."

"Dalton? But that's the Fair *Grossmütter* Jerusha was going to when she found you in the storm."

Jenny nodded. "I know. There are so many strange tie-ins. The little boy lost in a huge snowstorm, a little boy who had no one to save him like I had. The Quilt Fair, the Amish connection. It's just gotten hold of me and I've been thinking about it constantly. And then... I think your papa shared something with me."

"Papa?"

Jenny got up. "I have something I want to show you."

She walked into the bedroom and picked up the photograph from the dresser, then went back into the kitchen. She put it down on the table in front of Rachel. Rachel's mouth opened in surprise and then she giggled.

"That's you and Papa! But how young you were and... you're not wearing a *kappe!* And look at Papa. He looks like a hippie. And those crazy curls, Mama. Goodness. When and where was this taken?"

Jenny chuckled. "Your papa *was* a hippie, a total hippie. And I thought I was leaving Apple Creek and the Amish community forever. We were running away. We had fallen in love and your grandfather put me under the *Meidung.*"

"The *Bann?* Mama, you never told me about that. I'm seeing a whole new side of you. And what did Papa tell you?"

"Well, just look at the picture. Is that really your papa?"

"No. At least it's not the papa I knew."

"And that's just it. When your papa looked like that, he was lost, afraid, running away. But inside of him was a whole different person, someone who had a history, a family, courage..."

"Someone completely different."

"And then when your papa was in the boating accident and had amnesia for eight years..."

"He became someone different again," Rachel exclaimed.

Jenny nodded. "Richard Sandbridge. The people who found him named him after the place where the storm swept him ashore. And for eight years we thought he drowned."

Rachel frowned. "That was a hard time in my life, especially when we found him again."

"Yes, for me too. I knew three different Jonathans all in the same body. And as I was looking at the picture, the thought came to me. *Things are not always as they seem, Jenny.* And it was like Jonathan was telling me that the little boy in blue was lost, too. That he was running, trying to get home, but that the story of this little boy is not what it seems. There is something hidden... hidden and maybe dangerous, about this whole affair."

"I don't like the word dangerous, Mama."

"I know. I think that's just a feeling I have. Probably means nothing."

Rachel put the picture down. "So, where does the lady live who wrote the letter? Did she give you an address?"

"Yes, the letter's over there on the counter."

Rachel went to the counter and picked up the letter. "Centerville. The post office box address is in Centerville. That's just on the other side of Lancaster. It's only thirty minutes away. Did she give you a phone number?"

"No."

"Maybe we can find out more from the post office, a real address, and track her down—see if she's got any more information."

"We?"

Rachel was silent for a moment. "You are going to invite us to come stay with you in Apple Creek while you sort this one out for Elbert, aren't you, Mama? Daniel and I could do a lot of the footwork. And Daniel is a good bodyguard. He once saved me from a very dangerous situation. Very dangerous, remember?"

Jenny nodded and caressed her daughter's hair. "I remember, my darling. Your papa was there too…"

"And Uncle Bobby. Oh, let us come, Mama!"

"Well, I hoped you two would babysit the farm while I was gone."

"Why not have the boys do it? Your grandkids love this place and they are very responsible young men. I would love to visit Apple Creek again."

"Let me think about it. I admit you were a big help and…it was definitely nice having you with us the last time we went home."

Rachel smiled. "Home, eh? I thought this was your home."

Jenny shrugged. "You know what I mean. Apple Creek will always be home, no matter where I go."

"In the meantime, let's get Uncle Bobby to take us for a drive to Centerville."

A few hours later, Bobby, Jenny and Rachel were in the small town of Centerville, Pennsylvania, at the post office. Bobby showed the lady his ID and sheriff's association membership card. The postmistress looked doubtful.

"Well, Sheriff, we rarely give out private information…"

"This is an official murder investigation, ma'am, and this lady is presently our only link to the dead person's identity. If you have questions, you can call Detective Elbert Wainwright in Wooster, Ohio, and he will verify that we are working for him."

The woman nodded. "Do you have a number?"

Bobby reached in his wallet and pulled out Elbert's card. "This is his private line."

The woman went to the phone on the wall and dialed the number. In a moment, they heard Elbert's voice. "Detective Elbert Wainwright."

"Yes, I'm the postmistress of Centerville, Pennsylvania and I have Sheriff Bobby Halverson and Jenny Hershberger here asking me for some information they say is germane to a murder investigation. Can I give it to them?"

She listened for a moment and then nodded. "Thank you, Detective." The postmistress hung up and turned back to the counter. She opened a drawer and riffed through some cards. Finally, she found what she was looking for and pulled out a file card. "This is an old account for Roberta Kelley. It expired almost ten years ago. But it has the address." She jotted down the information and handed it to Bobby. They turned to go.

"Oh, Jenny..."

Jenny turned back. The woman was smiling and red-faced. "I'm a big fan of yours and I know about your books..." she glanced around and then whispered conspiratorially... "even though I know that someone else pretended to write them because you're Amish and you're not supposed to." She reached under the counter and pulled out a book—*A Quilt For Jenna*. "Would you sign this for me?" She blushed again.

Jenny stared at the book. It was the story of how her mother, Jerusha, found her in a terrible snowstorm while she was on the way to the Dalton Quilt Fair. Jenny took the book in trembling hands.

Gott, is this you showing me how connected I really am to this little boy?

BOBBY SLOWED DOWN AND LOOKED OVER. "OKAY, WE ARE ON Linton Road. What's the number?"

"Roberta Kelley, 2543 Linton Road."

Rachel pointed to a mailbox. "There's 2265. So, it's on this side of the road just three blocks up."

Bobby drove the old Ford down the street.

"2300 block, 2400 block, so here's 2501. It should be just a few houses up."

Bobby drove slowly down the block until he came to the mailbox that said 2543. He pulled over. There was a house, but it looked abandoned. Weeds crowded every inch of the yard, and there were lots of shingles missing from the roof. They got out of the car and walked up the sidewalk toward the front porch. Weed-filled cracks broke the concrete apart. They came to the front stairs. The board on the first step was missing, and they had to stretch over it to get onto the porch.

"No one lives here, Mama."

Jenny could see. The glass in the front door was missing and a piece of plywood covered the window. A litter of leaves and other debris filled the porch. Jenny looked at Bobby. "What do you make of this?"

Bobby grinned. "Looks like we missed her."

"Can I help you?"

They turned. An elderly man was standing out on the sidewalk.

Jenny walked down. "Yes, we are looking for Roberta Kelley. She gave me this house as her address."

The man spit part of the tobacco he was chewing on the grass. "Well, it don't take but one eye and half a brain to figger out they ain't nobody lives here."

"Yes, I can see that. Did Roberta Kelley ever live here?"

"Was a gal lived here about ten years ago, with her boyfriend. They was renting the place from old man Kooken. I think her name might have been Roberta—we called her Bobbie, but I don't remember her boyfriend's name. Fought all the time. He was a mean one. One day they was just gone, never seen'em again. Then Kooken died with no relatives and the house has been sitting here vacant ever since. That's all I know."

The old man whistled and a mangy old dog that had been doing his business in the side yard ambled out.

"Need anything else?"

Jenny watched as the old man and the dog ambled on down the street.

Why would she give me an address where she hadn't lived for ten years?

She dug in her purse and pulled out the letter from Roberta. The sender address was Centerville, but the postmark was Stroudsburg, Pennsylvania.

Stroudsburg! Why, that's where my birth mother is buried.

Then the thought came again.

Nothing is as it seems, Jenny...

6

WHO IS HE?

The trip to Ohio was uneventful. Elbert authorized an SUV and Bobby was having a great time playing chauffeur. Even at eighty-two, Bobby was fit and focused. Jenny had relented and asked Rachel and Daniel to come along, so suitcases and other necessities filled the back of the vehicle. The six-hour trip seemed to fly by. Jenny, in the back seat with Rachel, had been silent for a large part of the ride. Rachel leaned over and touched her mother's hand.

"Excited about being in the old house?"

Jenny nodded and squeezed Rachel's hand. "Yes, dearest. It's like *Gott* wants to put me in the one place where I always feel the safest and where it is most easy to solve my problems." She sighed. "When I was in my room at night in Apple Creek... when I was a little girl, I was never afraid, because my papa and mama were right in the next room. My papa was the rock in my life. And my mama..." She squeezed Rachel's hand. "Well, whenever I had a problem, I knew I would find the answer, because *Gott* always spoke to me through Papa and Mama. And if I had to really think something over, I would sit in the porch swing for hours. Eventually, I figured it out."

Rachel snuggled close to her mama. "*Grossdaddi* and *Gross-mütter* loved you so much, I could always tell. And when we went there after Papa Jonathan disappeared, I felt safe, and very loved, too."

Jenny felt the beat of her daughter's heart. She remembered being a child struggling with nightmares, especially the nightmare about being lost in the terrible snowstorm. She remembered when she would wake up terrified and her mother would come to her. She remembered...

*J*ENNY SAT UP IN BED AND SCREAMED.

"Mama, Mama, where are you? Come find me Mama."

There was the sound of hurried footsteps in the hall and then Jerusha came into the room holding a lamp.

"Jenny, darling, what is it?" she asked as she came to the side of Jenny's bed.

"A dream, Mama, a horrible dream," Jenny sobbed. "The snow, and the cold and...and the bad man."

Jerusha put the lamp on the stand by the bed and sat next to Jenny. She took the girl in her arms and kissed her forehead.

"I'm here, my darling, I'm here."

Jerusha held Jenny close and Jenny felt the beating of her mother's heart. Jenny clung even tighter to her mother. Her mother's arms had always been a haven for her, since the day Jerusha rescued her from the great snowstorm. Jerusha had kept Jenny alive by holding the child next to her heart throughout the long nights until Papa and Uncle Bobby had rescued them, and that was the earliest memory Jenny had of her mother. The steady beat of her mother's heart comforted her and it was always in this place of refuge and life that she felt the most secure...

· · ·

pulled a hanky out and wiped her eyes. Rachel looked at her. Jenny laughed. "Don't mind me, I get emotional sometimes, just thinking about my mama and the many blessings she brought to my life… about Apple Creek and the tiny but precious world of my childhood."

Bobby spoke from the front. "Apple Creek, Ohio, next exit. All ashore that's going ashore."

Back home.

Jenny loved this house. She walked slowly up the path to the front porch. Everything was just as it had always been. The paint, white and fresh on the clapboard siding, the fancy gingerbread scrollwork in between the porch posts, the handmade railing, the garden box along the front of the house where her mama had grown iris and gladiolas. Her cousin Jared stood on the porch.

"*Wie ghets,* Jenny! *Willkommen!* So good to see you again. *Auch das alte Haus heißt Sie herzlich willkommen.*"

Jenny nodded. "It almost seems like it is welcoming me, doesn't it? Everything is just the same. I so appreciate the care you take, Jared."

Jared reddened and scuffed his foot. "It is the least I can do for the Springers… and my favorite cousin."

Daniel and Bobby brought the big suitcases in and put them in the bedrooms. Jenny went into her old room and unpacked. When she finished, she came out to find Jared and his stout little wife, Evangeline, bustling about. The smell of strong *kaffee* and the delicious odor of meatloaf filled the kitchen and invaded her senses.

Evangeline, a plump little Amish woman with a lovely smile, was busy with a large pan of macaroni and cheese, and fresh string beans were boiling in a saucepan. There was another smell, too; a delicious Apple Creek smell.

"Apple cobbler, Evangeline?"

Vangie grinned. "*Ja,* Jenny. Apple cake from Apple Creek."

"It smells so good. Yum!"

Bobby wandered into the kitchen. "So, can I just get my plate out, find a chair, and wait? This kitchen is the most happening place in this little burg."

"*Ja,* Sheriff Bobby, but first you can bring me an armful of wood for the stove."

Bobby shrugged. "If that's the price I must pay, Vangie, then so be it." He headed out the back door toward the woodpile.

Dinner was soon ready, and they all sat down together. Once everyone sat, they quieted, then bowed their heads for a silent prayer. In a few moments, Jared cleared his throat, and they all pitched in with gusto. They were even quieter for a long time, except for the clicking of utensils on the plates and the quiet requests to pass this or that. Finally, the silence was broken by the scraping of Bobby's chair, and a low moan from Daniel.

Bobby shook his head. "Vangie, that was *sehr gut.*"

They all smiled at Bobby's German.

Daniel nodded and groaned again. "I think I need to get up and go lay on the couch."

"But Daniel, *wir haben den kuchen mit Sahne noch nicht gehabt!*"

Daniel scooted back up to the table. "Right, the apple cake and fresh cream. Not going anywhere just yet."

A large helping of cake and some fresh *kaffee* later, Jenny got up and started clearing the table.

Vangie shook her head. "*Nein,* Jenny. Tonight, you rest. I will finish in here."

Jenny put her arms around Vangie and hugged. "That's sweet of you, dear. I think I hear the porch swing calling. I have some things to think through."

THE SUN WAS GOING DOWN IN THE WEST AND LONG SHADOWS reached across the yard. There was a slight chill in the evening air, a portent of the coming of fall. Jenny slipped a warm shawl over her shoulders and wandered down the porch to the old swing. The big cushions were in place and she sank down.

This is what home means to me...

She thought of the many hours she had pondered the issues of her life right in this swing. Or the other times when Jonathan was courting her and they sat together in the gathering twilight talking about all the things yet to come in their lives.

As she sat, the picture of the little boy came into her mind— the blond hair, the blue denim shirt and jacket, the blue eyes. And the picture in her dresser, the house where nobody lived...

So many pieces going around in my head. Somehow, Gott has woven that boy's tragedy and my life together. Something about things not being as they seem. The snowstorm, the Dalton Quilt Fair, Jonathan and I running away and looking like Englischers.

Jenny bowed her head and whispered. "It's a puzzle, Lord. I guess I just must dig deeper and find out how all these things fit together."

And then, like the morning sun just breaking over the eastern hills, a scripture came to her.

For nothing is secret that will not be revealed, nor anything hidden that will not be known and come to light.

Jenny whispered again. "All right, Lord. I will let you lead the way. Help me keep out of your way."

ELBERT WAINWRIGHT SMILED AT THE PETITE, SILVER-HAIRED AMISH woman sitting on the other side of his desk. Jenny was in her sixties, but aside from some crow's feet around her eyes and lots of smile lines, her face was clear and still radiated the loveliness of her youth.

"So where do we start, Jenny?"

Jenny shrugged. "I have thought about it and I guess the first place we need to go is Shipshewana. That's where the woman, Roberta, said the grandmother lived. If she is a quilter and Amish, I can probably track her down."

Elbert grinned.

Yes, I'm sure you can.

"But this Roberta didn't turn out to be what she seemed, Jenny. I mean, the abandoned house, the letter addressed from there but postmarked from Stroudsburg. Quite a few red herrings already."

Jenny frowned. "That's true, Elbert, but I'm too deep into this to stop now."

Bobby reached for a Camel and then remembered he was trying to quit. "It won't hurt for us to drive up there. It's about a four-hour drive and the Amish community is very localized. We have the name of the *bischof* and his address. We'll go up, try to locate Amanda and if we run into a dead end, we turn around and come back. If not, we go talk with Amanda and see if she really is the boy's grandmother. Pretty cut and dried."

"Oh, don't mistake me. I want you to go. For some reason, this case has dug its claws into me, too—I think about it all the time. And when I heard Jenny's connection to the story, well, I just had a feeling we will somehow understand all this. So, off you go to Shipshewana. Just keep me informed."

Jenny stood up. "If there is something to find in Indiana, we'll find it."

"I know you will, Jenny. I have absolutely no doubt of that."

7

AMANDA

Bobby and Jenny pulled into the courtyard at the Blue Gate Inn in Shipshewana after their drive up from Wooster. The big sign over the door said Restaurant and Bakery.

Bobby nodded. "That's my favorite kind of sign. Let's go investigate, detective."

Gathering up their travel bags, they walked into the lobby. Off to the right was a large dining room. Against the back wall of the room was a buffet where people were lining up to get plates and then working their way down through the wide variety of delicious looking dishes.

Bobby pointed. "As soon as we get checked in, that's where I'm headed."

"What?"

"I'm headed for the buffet."

"Oh, right. Sounds good."

Bobby looked at Jenny. "You okay, girl?"

Jenny shook her head. "Sorry, Bobby. I am pre-occupied with all this. Yes, let's check in and go eat."

They walked up to the front desk. The man behind the counter seemed bemused by the eclectic but interesting couple standing there—a petite older Amish woman and an old but obviously fit military type guy. He smiled. "Can I help you?"

"Yes, we have a reservation for two single rooms. Jenny Hershberger and Bobby Halverson."

The clerk scanned the computer screen. "Yes, here you are. Can I see a driver's license?" He smiled at Jenny. "Not yours, of course, his." He nodded toward Bobby, who pulled out his wallet and handed over his license.

"Thanks."

The clerk entered the information and then handed over two key cards. "We are putting you in our Shipshewana Kings, Room 121 and 122, right across the hall from each other." He pointed to the left, where there was a staircase and a hallway. "Go down the hall to the left." He nodded to a nice-looking young woman standing nearby. "Janie, would you help these folks?"

Janie grabbed a cart, loaded their bags, and started off. "This way please, it's not too far."

Jenny stopped for a moment and turned to the clerk. "I'm looking for a woman here in town. I don't know her last name, but she's Amish, and she's a quilter."

The clerk smiled. "Well, then you should do the Barn Quilt tour. Every place in town that sells or exhibits quilts is on the tour, plus all the quilt outlets in the six little towns right around Shipshewana. Someone on the tour should know her. Here, take this." He reached under the counter and pulled out a pamphlet. "This is a self-guided tour map. It shows all the Barn Quilt sites in LaGrange County. It starts right down the street at Prough Farms and takes you to all the quilt barns, and all the shops where they display Amish quilts."

Jenny took the map gratefully. "Thank you, ah…"

"James."

"Thank you, James. This is most helpful."

Four hours later they had been to Prough Farms, The Amish Log Cabin, The Shipshewana Campground, Franks, The Village View, Weiland/Keffer, FBI Farms and The Tingley Farm. They had discovered exactly nothing in their search. Nobody knew of a quilter named Amanda in the area. Their next stop was the little village of Mongo, about 20 miles from Shipshewana. They pulled into the parking lot at The Trading Post Canoe Rental and Campground. There was a big barn there with a large Barn Quilt placard hanging on the wall. Jenny got out of the car and looked at the barn. Her shoulders slumped.

"Tired?"

Jenny looked over at her friend. "Yes, and discouraged. The Amish quilting community is a tight group. Usually everyone knows everyone. But nobody knows Amanda. Maybe Roberta Kelley, whoever she is, led us on a complete wild goose chase. After all, she sent us to an abandoned house."

"Well, remember that the incident with Amanda at the Dalton Fair happened eleven years ago. And all the people we have spoken to were young. Maybe Amanda is from a different generation. There are a lot of stops on this map, so we may be here a few more days. Let's just see what happens."

Jenny took hold of Bobby's arm. "You're right, Uncle Bobby. We are here and let's redeem the time."

There was a store next to the barn with a sign in the window —Genuine Amish Quilts. They walked up some wooden steps and into the shop. All around them were quilts—large and small, all designs and colors, hanging from walls, displayed on racks, and folded in piles. A voice called out from somewhere in the back.

"Be right with you."

A moment later, a white-haired woman came out from between two rows of shelves piled high with quilts.

"May I help you?"

Jenny nodded. "I hope so. We are looking for an Amish

quilter named Amanda. She is from Shipshewana, or the surrounding area. She would probably be in her mid to late sixties. We hoped that someone in the quilting community might know of her."

"I don't know anybody by that name. Of course, I've only been in the Shipshewana area for a few months. I moved up from Indianapolis. Why are you looking for her?"

Bobby stepped forward and showed the woman his ID. "I'm former sheriff Bobby Halverson, and this is Jenny Hershberger. We are working on a cold case investigation with Detective Elbert Wainwright from Wooster, Ohio." He handed the woman one of Elbert's cards. "It involves the Boy In Blue Denim case. Perhaps you are familiar with that story."

The woman nodded slowly. "Yes, I remember that from when it happened. A little boy found dead in the snow over east, about ten years ago."

"That's the one."

"And what does this Amanda have to do with the case and... uh..." she looked at Jenny, "... isn't it unusual for an Amish woman to be working as a detective?"

Jenny smiled. "Yes, indeed it is unusual, and the elders of my church back in Paradise, Pennsylvania, were a little concerned, too. But Bobby... Sheriff Halverson... is an old family friend, and he makes sure I am well protected and stay on the straight and narrow."

Bobby grinned. "As much as possible."

"Perhaps you remember Emma Johnson, the girl they found buried in the box in Jepson's woods back in Apple Creek."

The woman brightened. "Oh, certainly. You're the Jenny Hershberger who solved that case?"

"Well, I helped, but it took a lot of work by Elbert, Bobby, and others, and, of course, the Lord stepped in from time to time." Jenny smiled.

The woman looked around. "My name is Jane Thompson and I've never met a genuine celebrity. Would you like some coffee?"

Jenny reddened. "I certainly don't think of myself that way, but thank you. And yes, we would love some. It's been a long day already."

"Give me a minute. It's on a hotplate in the back. Do you use cream?"

Bobby nodded. "Yes, ma'am."

"Call me Jane." She pointed to the back of the shop. "There are some tables over there where people eat lunch. I'll meet you there."

In a few minutes, Jane came bustling up with a tray holding three cups of steaming coffee and a pitcher of cream. There was a plate of brownies to go with it. Jane sat down.

"Tell me more about Amanda."

Jenny put down her cup. "I write a column for my local paper about the Amish community and everything that goes on there. When Detective Wainwright had a friend put out a feature on cold cases in the Tri-state area of Indiana, Ohio and Pennsylvania, the Boy In Blue Denim was the lead story. Our local paper picked it up. I got a letter from a woman in the area who claimed to have met the boy's grandmother at the Dalton Quilt Fair just outside of Apple Creek, Ohio. She said the woman showed her a picture that matched the picture in the article. She didn't get the woman's last name, but told me she was Amish and from Shipshewana. It seemed like a slim lead, but because of the circumstances... meeting at the Dalton Fair, the woman being Amish, and a little boy lost in a snowstorm... all of which have a great deal of significance for me, well, when I contacted Detective Wainwright we agreed that Bobby and I should at least look into it."

Jane looked thoughtful. "Well, I don't know an Amanda, but if anybody does, it would be Granny Eckert."

"Who's that?"

"Granny Eckert has been around these parts all her life. She's a skilled Amish quilter herself and she knows everyone who is involved in the quilting community in this entire part of the state."

Bobby reached into his pocket and pulled out a pad. "Do you have an address?" He pushed the pad and pencil across the table.

"Surely. Granny lives out on North County Road." She jotted it down. "Go out and keep driving in the direction you were going—down Indiana 3 for about two hundred yards. You will come to East 325 North. Take a left and go about a half a mile. You will come to a 'T' intersection. Take a left onto North County Road and go about a mile. Granny's place is on the left with white fences and a big red Indiana style barn in the back. You will see beautiful iris flowers all along her fence. Can't miss it. Just go up and tell her Jane Thompson sent you."

Jenny took Jane's hand. "Thank you, Jane. Let's hope Granny Eckert can help us."

"Yes. And please, Jenny, won't you keep me informed about how it all works out? Just drop me a note here at the shop."

"Most certainly."

Granny Eckert's house was just as Jane had described it. Beautifully kept, green grass lawn rolling up to a white house on a small knoll. Large buckeye trees surrounded the house and a few stubborn iris lined the fence. The barn in back had a fresh bright coat of red paint. Bobby pulled in to the circular drive that led right up to the front steps. They stopped and got out. As they were looking at the house, the front screen opened. A tiny woman, probably just over five feet tall, came out. She wore older style Amish clothing—no buttons, only hooks—with her white hair pulled back in a severe bun under her *kappe* and a pair of square spectacles perched on her nose.

"Well, don't just stand their gawking. Come on up." Her eyes twinkled behind her glasses.

"Granny Eckert?"

"No one else, girl."

"Jane Thompson at the Genuine Amish Quilts store sent us."

"Oh, she did, did she? Now, what's that woman up to?"

"Jane thought you could help us find someone."

"I don't hear so good. You'll have to come up on the porch and have some lemonade and cookies. That is one thing that improves my hearing."

"Mine too," Bobby said.

"Ah, a kindred spirit. Come, come, we're burning daylight."

Jenny and Bobby went up on the porch while Granny disappeared through the screen door. In a moment, she was back with a tray—lemonade and cookies.

"I keep it handy because people are always dropping by." She motioned toward a table at the end of the porch. "Sit, sit."

They all sat down as Granny poured the lemonade. Once they settled, Granny Eckert pushed her glasses up on her nose. "Now, how can I help you?"

Jenny pulled out the letter from Roberta Kelley. "We are investigating what the police call a cold case..."

"A case that's been sitting on the back burner for a long time."

Jenny nodded. "That's right. This one involves a little boy murdered and left in the snow a long time ago. They have never identified him. We think the boy's grandmother may live in this area. Her name is Amanda, and she's Amish and a quilter."

"Do you have a picture of the boy?"

Jenny reached in her bag and pulled out the folder, and handed the pictures of the boy over.

Granny looked them over and then nodded. "Well, her given name is Amanda, but we all call her Mandy, Mandy Beier."

Jenny's mouth opened, then shut. "You know her?"

"Well, if it's who I think it is, yes, I know her."

"Why haven't any of the other quilters heard of her?"

"Oh, those young whippersnappers know nothing. I've known Mandy all her life. She was a great quilter. It's a very sad story. She lost her daughter to cancer and then her grandson and son-in-law kind of went missing. She hasn't heard from them for ten years. Then right after that, Mandy's husband died. The whole thing shook her up so bad she just withdrew. She stopped quilting, stays at home, and never goes out except to the store. So that's why the young'uns don't know her." She looked at the picture again. "I'm not sure, but I think this little boy might be her missing grandson. Is that why you're here?"

Jenny shrugged. "Yes. A woman who sent me a letter said she met Amanda at a quilting fair and Amanda showed her a picture of her grandson. It was very similar to the picture of the little boy in these pictures. The newspapers called him The Boy In Blue Denim."

"I remember that story. They found him over near the Ohio State line. I never thought to put it together with Mandy's grandson. Oh, the whole thing with Mandy was all very strange." Granny Eckert got up. "Well, we best get going."

Bobby smiled. "Where are we going?"

"Why, over to see Mandy, you big moose. She lives just down the road."

8
___

FOUND

Bobby followed Granny's instructions and in just a few minutes, they were turning down a long lane off North County Road. The road to the house was gravel and rutted. Jenny noticed they had not pruned the old chestnut trees on either side of the road for a long time, and many dead branches marred their graceful lines. Broken pickets marred the fence along both sides of the road, and what part of the fence remained standing was badly in need of a coat of white paint. They pulled around the last turn and drew up before the house. The front door screen hung askew on one hinge and weeds ruled what appeared to be the front yard. Swallow's nests marred the gingerbread trim above the porch rail and a broken pane in the front window gaped like a missing tooth.

Granny sighed. "Very sad. Mandy used to be such a lively girl. This farm was a showplace, and her husband, Mervin, kept it up immaculately. When her daughter Eliza died, Eliza's husband went to work in Texas, and Mandy only saw him one and her grandson one more time. Then a tree fell on Mervin out in the woods yonder..." she pointed to a fringe of woods along the back fence, "and Mandy just quit. She goes into town once a month, but she avoids everyone and just gets what she needs and then comes home. She won't let anybody on the place but me, and that's only because I taught her how to quilt."

Bobby pulled the SUV up in front of the porch. A raggedy-looking cat scampered away when they got out, and several crows cawed mournfully from a bare tree beside the house.

"She just let everything go. She sits inside all day and never comes out, except for her once-a-month trip to town. Wait here."

Granny Eckert walked up the stairs and knocked on the door. "Mandy? Mandy, it's Granny Eckert. I need to talk to you."

She waited for a few minutes and then she knocked again. "Mandy, Mandy..."

Just then the front door opened a crack. Jenny heard a soft voice.

"What is it, Granny? And who are those people?"

"I'm sorry to disturb you, honey, but these people need to speak with you. It's about your grandson."

"What about him?"

"Can we come in and talk? Just for a few minutes. They are nice people and they are here to help."

The door closed and Jenny heard the chain lock slide off. Then the door opened. "Come in, Granny. And... and bring your friends."

Granny motioned to Bobby and Jenny and they went up the stairs and into the house.

"Come into the living room." Amanda led the way down a long hall. A flight of stairs on the left led up to the second floor. The hallway was dim, lit only by a single bulb in a wall fixture. The bulb did little to dispel the darkness. Amanda came to the living room and motioned them to go in. The room was dark, except for a small amount of light coming in around the closed blinds. There was a couch and several chairs. Amanda turned on a floor lamp by the couch and motioned for Jenny to sit. Amanda and Granny sat on the couch with Jenny and Bobby sat in a chair across from them.

"What about my grandson?"

Jenny looked at Amanda. She was pale, dressed in black, and her hair was in a severe bun under her *kappe*. Her eyes were dark, and Jenny could sense the genuine pain in the woman. She reached out her hand. Amanda took it like a drowning woman takes hold of a rope.

"Amanda, I'm Jenny Hershberger and this is Sheriff Bobby Halverson, and we want to ask you some questions... and yes, it's about your grandson."

Amanda nodded.

Jenny went on. "About ten years ago, they found a little boy dead in the snow over by the Ohio State line. Nobody knew who he was. The newspapers called him The Boy In Blue Denim. A month ago, a friend of ours, Detective Elbert Wainwright, was going through some old files and the case caught his attention. He had a friend of his run a story and several papers across the tri-state area picked it up. A newspaper I write a column for in Paradise, Pennsylvania, ran the story. A woman in the area saw the story and sent me a letter at the paper. She had seen the photo of the boy and said that she met you at the Dalton Quilt Fair near Apple Creek years before, and that you showed her a picture that was very similar to the boy in the picture. She remembered your first name, Amanda, and that you were from this area. Because Bobby and I had helped Detective Wainwright with another case in the Amish community, he asked us if we would come out here and see if we could find the Amanda this woman mentioned. We have been searching all day, and fortunately, it seems *Gott* led us to Granny Eckert and Granny brought us here. We would like to find out if you know this boy. Would you be all right with that?"

Amanda looked over at Granny Eckert, who nodded, and then turned back to Jenny.

"Yes. That would be fine."

Jenny reached into her bag and pulled out the folder with the pictures. She pulled out the closeup of the little boy and handed it to Amanda.

Amanda gasped and put her hand over her mouth. She looked at the picture for just a moment and then turned away. Then she asked softly. "Did he have anything with him?"

Jenny nodded. "A first grade reader and..."

"A rainbow-colored toy horse?"

Jenny nodded. "Yes, a rainbow-colored horse."

Amanda sighed. "It's Danny."

Another deep sigh. Then she handed the picture back. "So, he's dead then?"

Jenny nodded.

"Well, at least now I know." She put her face in her hands and wept. Her shoulders shook with the sobs. Jenny leaned over and took Amanda in her arms. They sat that way for a long, long time.

After a while, the sobs grew weaker and Amanda collected herself. Granny slipped her a handkerchief and she wiped her eyes.

Jenny sat back. "Can you tell us about him?"

Amanda nodded. "His name is Danny Wittmer. He's the son of my daughter, Eliza and her husband, Levon Wittmer. The last time we saw him was when he and his father stopped by on their way back from Texas."

"Texas?"

"That's a long story. But first, tell me how you got involved in all this."

Jenny hesitated. "Well, when I saw the picture of the little boy and heard the details, the story just resonated with me and somehow I felt I had to get involved."

Amanda looked at Jenny. "Why?"

"That is also a long story."

"Go ahead."

Jenny glanced over at Bobby, who nodded for her to continue.

Jenny shifted on the couch to face Amanda. "When I was three years old, an Amish couple in Apple Creek, Ohio, adopted me. How I got to Apple Creek is the strange part. Before I was born, my birth mother, Rachel Borntraeger, who was also Amish, got involved with an *Englischer* and got pregnant. Her *daed*, who was a *bischof* in Paradise, Pennsylvania, kicked her out of the house. The man she was involved with, my birth father, Robert St. Clair, was the son of an extremely wealthy family. He loved my mother very much and married her. When I was born, Robert's father disowned him and Robert went to work for a living. Then, he was killed in a terrible car accident. My birth mother had no one to turn to, so she went to New York to see Robert's parents. I was three then. By that time Robert's father had died from a heart attack and when my mother, Rachel, went to the house on Park Avenue, Robert's sister-in-law, a very wicked woman who wanted no competition for the inheritance, had my mother threatened and thrown out of her hotel. While she was on the streets, Robert's sister-in-law put her in the clutches of a very evil man. The man got my mother addicted to drugs, and she died from an overdose."

Jenny stopped and took a deep breath, then continued.

"The man was running away from a bank robbery and going to California when my mother died in Stroudsburg, Pennsylvania. Just outside of Apple Creek, Ohio, he ran into the biggest blizzard in Ohio history. He crashed his car, and it slid onto a frozen pond and while he was trying to get out of the car, he fell through the ice and drowned. So, I was all alone in the back of the car in the heart of a huge snowstorm. While that was happening, the woman who became my adoptive mother, Jerusha Springer, was on her way to the same Quilt Fair in Dalton, where the woman who wrote to me said she met you. My mama was a master quilter, and she was taking her finest quilt to show at the fair. Her car slid off the road on the way and her driver went to get help. He was injured in the storm and no one knew where my mama was. While trying to get to safety, she found me in the wrecked car. She carried me to a cabin in the woods and kept me there for three days while her husband, my adoptive papa Rueben, and my Uncle Bobby..." she nodded at Bobby... "searched day and night for us. My mother saved me by wrapping me in her beautiful quilt and holding me next to her body to keep me warm. When I read about a little boy lost in a terrible storm and the letter came about you being at the Quilt Fair in Dalton, I just felt like I had to do something for the boy. He did not have anyone to save him from the storm like I had, and my heart went out to him. That's why I got involved."

"Oh my," Granny Eckert said.

Jenny took Amanda's hands. "This part of the story will be hard, Amanda. What I didn't tell you was that someone murdered Danny."

Amanda's eyes went wide. "Murdered!"

"Yes. I know that's hard to hear. Somebody smothered him to death in a shed off a rural path in eastern Indiana. No one knows how he got there or who he was with."

Amanda's face had gone pale.

"You said the last time you saw him, he was returning from Texas with his father. Do you think his father could have had anything to do with Danny's death?"

"No, no. Levon Wittmer was a good man. He loved Danny. He loved my daughter. He would never do such a thing."

"Well, I want to say this. I believe *Gott* has asked me to get involved to find justice for Danny. I promise you that Bobby and I and our friend, Detective Wainwright, will do everything in our power to bring Danny's killer to justice."

Amanda smiled a weak smile. "Thank you, Jenny."

"Now, tell us about Eliza and Levon... and Danny. Tell us everything."

65

9

ELIZA—APRIL, 1982

Eliza Beier stepped off the train at the station in Smicksburg, Pennsylvania. She looked around for her cousin, Grace, but didn't see her. Her heart beat a little faster than normal because she was away from her home in Indiana for the very first time. She had never traveled farther than Shipshewana, which was only fifteen miles away from her home. Grace had invited her to come for the summer and although it wasn't really time for her *rumspringa,* her mama felt it would be good for Eliza to see a little more of the world. So here she was in Smicksburg, waiting for her cousin.

"Excuse me miss, are you Eliza Beier?"

Eliza turned around and stared into the chest of a tall young man. She looked up to see a very handsome face, surrounded by longish, curly black hair. He was obviously Amish and sported no beard, which meant he was single. "Are these your bags?"

He had some bags on a dolly and it looked like they were all hers.

Eliza nodded.

The tall man smiled. "I'm Levon Wittmer. I'm a friend of your cousin, Grace. Coming into town today, I found her alongside the road. It seems the wheel on her buggy came loose. I volunteered to come fetch you." He nodded at the bags. "I checked the tags on your luggage. I think they are all here."

Eliza counted the bags. "Yes... they... uh... seem to all be here."

"Good. Let's go pick up Grace and get you both to home. She's waiting with her horse and buggy—about a mile from here."

Eliza hesitated. "But how do I know..."

"...if I'm not a kidnapper or some weirdo?" He laughed, and it was deep and alive and a small thrill went down Eliza's back. "Gracie thought you might be suspicious, so she told me to say this—Perticket."

"Perticket?"

"Yes, that's the name of your cat, isn't it?"

"Oh... ah... why, yes... Perticket. My cat. Yes... my cat." Eliza felt her face burning.

Levon grinned. "And only Gracie would know that, right?"

Eliza nodded.

"Well, now that we have established my *bona fides,* let's go."

Levon pushed the cart across the platform to a wagon hitched under a tree. Two beautiful chocolate-colored mares stood in the traces.

Eliza couldn't take her eyes off the wonderful horses. "Why, they are lovely!"

Levon reddened, but smiled. "Yes, they are. They are pure-bred Morgan horses. My papa and I own a horse farm and we raise them. They are the best working horses of all the breeds, except for maybe the Percherons." He lifted the bags into the back and then offered Eliza a hand up. "*Kumme, bis Sie gehen!*"

Eliza felt the strength of him in his grip and his arm.

I didn't know what this summer was going to be like, but now...

She reddened at the thought and turned her face.

Levon hadn't noticed. He chucked the reins, and the horses stepped off in a smart trot. "Let's go find Grace."

Eliza looked skyward. *Maybe I have already found grace...*

THAT NIGHT AFTER DINNER AT GRACE'S HOUSE, THE GIRLS SAT IN Grace's bedroom getting ready for bed. Eliza took out the pins holding her bun in place and combed out her long, blond hair. It fell softly around her shoulders.

Her cousin smiled. "Levon likes you."

Eliza felt a hot rush of blood suffuse her face. Grace giggled. "Why, Eliza! You like him too."

"Don't be silly, Gracie. I don't even know him."

Gracie folded her hands and put them up by her cheeks. She collapsed on the bed with an enormous sigh. "Love at first sight. Oh, I've always heard of it, but to see it right before my eyes. Oh, Eliza!"

Eliza jumped on her brash cousin. "You stop that. I'm hardly old enough to court."

Grace pulled her into a warm embrace. The two girls lay together on the bed. "Eliza, you deserve the best, and Levon Wittmer is the best around here by a long shot."

"But what about you? Surely you have set your *kappe* for him?"

Gracie shrugged. "Levon let me know a long time ago that we could never be more than friends. So friends we are and I am the better for it."

"He said he and his father raise those beautiful horses."

"That's true, Eliza. They have a wonderful farm about three miles from here. Would you like to go visit?"

Eliza buried her face in the comforter.

"Eliza! You do like him."

"No, I don't. Come on, Gracie, stop tormenting me."

"Come on, let's go to bed. You can gather up your emotions by the morning and be cool, calm, and collected when we take a drive and just happen to go past the Wittmer farm. You'll love it."

The next morning, after breakfast, the girls took the drive. Gracie almost had to shove Eliza into the buggy. It was a beautiful day in early June and the fields around Smicksburg were green with crops. The farms were as immaculate as the farms in Shipshewana. Corn was growing in perfect rows and the Amish homes were beautifully kept and cared for. Red oaks and shagbark hickory trees lined the road. They stayed off to the right side, but there weren't many cars passing, so Eliza had time to focus on the scenery.

"Papa got the wheel all straightened out, so we won't have the problem I had yesterday."

Eliza stayed still, entranced by the lovely countryside. Pictures came into her head—Levon Wittmer taking her hand and helping her into his wagon... Levon Wittmer picking up her heavy trunk like it weighed nothing and placing it carefully in the back... Levon Wittmer speaking softly to his beautiful horses as they drove... Levon Wittmer...

"You're awfully quiet, Eliza. Thinking of something... of someone?" Gracie gave Eliza a soft elbow in the ribs.

"No... ah, yes... no... Oh Gracie, don't. Yes, I was thinking about him. He's very handsome and very nice, but I am not just going to show up at his farm and declare my undying love after just meeting him. Give me a chance to get to know him, for goodness' sake."

"Levon Wittmer is the kindest, gentlest, handsomest boy for fifty miles around. It's okay to fall in love with him. He won't play with your heart. He's straightforward. If he doesn't want to get serious, he will let you down gently. That's just the kind of man he is. Whoa, here we are."

Gracie turned her horse and buggy into a nicely shaded lane. Many beautiful horses filled the white-fenced fields on both sides of the lane. They showed interest in the new arrivals, and a few came to the fence to watch Eliza and Grace drive by.

"They know my horse. Papa got him from Levon after Levon raised him right in these fields."

The drive opened into a spacious barnyard. The three-story house sat over to the left, surrounded by green lawn and shade trees. Straight ahead was a large red Pennsylvania barn, and to the right was a large training ring. Levon was working with a horse in the middle of the ring. Another man leaned against the fence and watched. Grace pulled the buggy up and stopped. Levon saw them and reined in the horse who was walking in a fast trot at the end of a long lead. He waved and walked over to the man standing at the fence. Levon pointed toward Gracie and Eliza and then he took hold of the top rail of the ring and vaulted over in a smooth, easy move. The two men walked over to the buggy.

"*Güten morgen*, Grace." Levon turned to Eliza, and she thought she saw his eyes light up. "*Güten morgen*, Eliza. *Wie gehts?*"

"*Güten morgen*, Levon. I am fine. It's a beautiful day and Gracie is showing me the sights. *Deine Pferde sind so schön.*"

The man with Levon smiled and nodded. "The best in Pennsylvania, except for maybe the horses on King Farm."

Levon threw an arm lock around the man's shoulders. "Ladies, I am being impolite. This is my best friend, Daniel King. He and his father own a Morgan horse farm in Paradise. He labors under the false assumption that the King horses are more beautiful than those here at Wittmer Farm. I'm not sure how to convince him otherwise."

Daniel King nodded. "Levon hasn't told you that the Wittmers got their first Morgan, Black King, from the King farm, but the

Wittmers have made some improvements on the line that some people might think put them ahead of us…

Levon grinned and applied more pressure.

Daniel rolled out of the armlock and held out his hand to the girls. "Daniel King."

Gracie took his hand. "Grace Miller. And this is my cousin, Eliza Beier."

"Pleased to meet you."

Daniel was almost as tall as Levon, with blonde hair, blue eyes, and was also extremely handsome.

Levon grinned. "Don't get your hopes up, girls. Daniel's spoken for back in Paradise."

Daniel smiled. "I wish someone would tell Rachel that."

Just then, the back door of the farmhouse opened, and a matronly looking woman peeked out. "Levon," she shouted, "don't just stand there. Ask the girls in for *kaffee und kaffee kuchen*" She started to go in and then turned. "You can come too, Daniel."

Levon pushed Daniel ahead. "You're lucky. Mama likes you." He turned to Eliza. "She'll like you, too."

⸻

THE SUMMER FLEW BY. ELIZA SPENT MORE TIME AT THE WITTMER farm and by the end of August, Eliza knew she wanted Levon to ask about courting. Finally, two days before she left, Levon pulled her aside.

"I need to talk to you."

"I was wondering if you were going to."

Levon clasped his hands together nervously. "Eliza, I've waited a long time and now I'll just come right out and say it. I am in love with you and want to ask your parents if I can court you."

Eliza took his hands in hers and stopped the nervous movement. "I feel the same way. But how will we do it? I live in Indiana. You will have to meet my parents. The *bischof* here will have to contact mine. Oh, it just seems so hard."

Levon pulled her close. "Do you really love me, Eliza?"

She nodded against his chest. "Yes."

"Then we can work it out. You go home and I will write. We'll talk about all the things we need to know about each other with nothing held back. Then I will come and meet your parents. We will be married next fall."

"A whole year? We have to wait…"

Levon took her by the shoulders and looked straight into her eyes. "Don't you want to be sure? Maybe this is just one of those summer romances. Maybe we were carried away by being together and having fun, and getting to know each other a bit. If we can wait a year, and still know we love each other, then won't it be worth it?"

She nodded. "You are right. Maybe when I get home, back to my routine, in my home, maybe I won't…"

Levon looked at her.

And then Eliza knew. Levon Wittmer was the man for her. And she would love him forever.

10

FINDING THE WAY

Mandy wiped her eyes with Granny's handkerchief. "That's how they met. Eliza wrote and told me all about it after she had been there for a week. They loved each other from the first. Eliza came home and then Levon came out after harvest and spoke to us. Mervin liked him right away. Levon was gentle and respectful. He treated Eliza with such kindness." She took Jenny's hand. "You don't think Levon could have done this, do you, Jenny?"

Jenny glanced over at Bobby, who shrugged. Jenny shook her head. "Except for finally finding out who the little lost boy is, we know exactly nothing about this case, especially about who might have killed Danny."

Mandy looked around at her guests and stood up. She wiped her eyes again and forced a smile. "I don't know what's gotten into me. Where are my manners? I just put a pot of *kaffee* on the stove before you arrived. Can I offer some?"

Bobby nodded. "That sounds great," and Jenny agreed.

Granny Eckert stood, too. "Let me help you, Mandy."

The two women left the room.

Bobby smiled at Jenny. "We seem to have made a bit of progress today."

"Yes. Actually, enormous progress. We know the identity of the boy, but..."

Bobby cut in. "We do not know how he got to the murder site. We don't know where his father, Levon, is. We have no idea what part Roberta Kelly plays in all this. And, worst of all, we don't have the faintest idea who might have killed Danny." Bobby shrugged. "This is the point in the investigation where we should make a list of suspects... but we don't have any suspects, except for Levon."

Jenny shook her head. "I don't know, Bobby, a lot of dead ends already. I guess we just find out as much as we can about Levon and Eliza and Danny, and go from there."

Just then Mandy and Granny Eckert came back with a tray, which she set on a table in front of the couch. The porcelain pot gave forth a steaming smell of strong *kaffee,* and there were cups on saucers and a pitcher of cream. Mandy poured everyone a cup and then sat down.

Jenny took a sip and then got the ball rolling again. "Tell us more about Danny, Mandy."

"He was such a sweet boy..." Mandy paused. "Although..."

"Although?"

Mandy looked away. She almost whispered her next words. "Danny was different as a little boy, very different. The doctor said he was autistic. I had never heard of that. I knew Eliza had a very difficult delivery when Danny was born. The umbilical cord wrapped around Danny's neck and his oxygen was reduced. The doctor said it affected his brain."

Bobby leaned forward. "When did they notice Danny was autistic?"

"From what Eliza told me in her letters, he avoided eye contact from shortly after he was born. He wasn't responding to his name by the time he was nine months old. He showed no facial expressions. He sat quietly and never sang or danced. He would come back to the world when he was with his mother and through her efforts he learned to read, and speak and get along somewhat. The doctor diagnosed him positively when he was four."

Jenny put her cup down. "It sounds like when your grandson could be reached, he was quite capable of interacting with people."

Mandy nodded. "Some people, his mama mostly, but Levon could reach him too. Like I said, he was very smart, he just was in a different world most of the time. Then, when his mama died, he retreated almost completely into himself. He didn't talk to people, just to Horse."

Jenny looked closely at Mandy. "Is Horse the toy horse they found with Danny?"

"Yes. Danny had two things that mattered to him in this world, Horse, and his first-grade reader."

Jenny nodded. "Yes, On Cherry Street, The Ginn Basic Reader. The one they found with him. I remember that book from when I was a little girl. Tom and Betty and their little dog."

Bobby smiled. "I remember the monkey from the front cover."

"Eliza gave him the book when he was very young. She had it when she was a little girl. She read it to him over and over. When Danny didn't start speaking as soon as he should have, the doctor suspected autism. He told Eliza autistic children have brief attention spans, so the short, little Cherry Street stories were perfect for him. Danny loved the stories and he would ask Eliza to read them repeatedly. His mama was the only one who could draw him out that way. Then my husband and I sent him Horse for Christmas when he was four. Eliza said it was the first thing that ever perfectly captured his attention. From then on, he was never without Horse and his book. One day Eliza found him reading to Horse in the closet."

Jenny smiled. "The closet?"

Mandy nodded. "Yes, and with the lights off. Eliza heard him and she listened through the door. He had memorized the book and was quoting it to Horse. Oh, Danny wasn't retarded, he was quite smart. He was just extremely shy and withdrawn."

"Jenny sipped her *kaffee.*

Bobby leaned forward. "Tell us more about Eliza and Levon."

"Like I said, Eliza and Levon met in the summer of 1982. Levon came in the fall to ask if he could court Eliza. It was a long-distance romance, of course, and mostly they just wrote letters, but Levon visited as much as he could and spent time with us. Most of it he spent with Mervin, getting to know him better. Eliza had not been in her *rumspringa* when she went to visit Gracie, but I encouraged her to find out more about the world. But she was a good Amish girl and didn't like what the other kids her age were doing. When she came home, she asked to be baptized into the church. Levon had already been baptized, so by spring we accepted they were to be married. I planted a celery patch." She took a deep breath and then went on.

"They were married that fall; November, 1983. Eliza was seventeen, Levon was twenty. Eliza moved to Smicksburg. After that she came to visit twice a year. She was very good to write us every week but after she moved we only saw her at those times. She got pregnant quickly and Danny was born in 1984. She always brought Danny with her when she came to visit. He was so quiet. He'd just look around with those big blue eyes. It was as though he was observing life but not taking part. But he loved us, I could tell. He knew we loved his mama, and we loved him, and that made us lovable."

"Tell them about Levon's parents," Granny said.

"Both of Levon's parents died within two years after he and Eliza were married, and Levon inherited the horse farm. That would have been in 1986."

"You said Eliza died. When did that happen?"

Mandy took a deep breath. "She died in 1993. She got sick.

Cancer. She might have had a chance if they had only taken her to a medical doctor."

Jenny had a memory. "That sounds like Jenna."

"Who is Jenna?"

"Jenna was my older sister. She died before I came to live with Mama Jerusha and Papa Reuben. I told you my mama was on the way to the Quilt Fair in Dalton when she was caught in the big storm and then found me. She was going there because she made an exquisite quilt she was entering in the competition. She knew she was going to win and when she did, she would take the prize and leave the Amish and Apple Creek behind."

Mandy looked puzzled. "Why would she do that?"

Jenny sighed. "My papa was one of the Amish men who left the church to fight in World War II." Jenny nodded at Bobby.

Bobby cleared his throat. "Her papa and I fought together at Henderson Field on Guadalcanal. Reuben won the Congressional Medal of Honor in that battle. He won it by saving his entire platoon and keeping the Japs... the Japanese from sweeping over the ridge. He stopped them with his bare hands in a trench at the top of the hill." Bobby took a deep breath and went on. "The problem was, it was so traumatic that Reuben went back to the church and swore he would never violate the *Ordnung* again. He became a strict legalist and would have nothing to do with the world. When his little girl, Jenna, got bacterial meningitis, he would not take her to the hospital. I literally had to tear her out of his arms and rush her to emergency, but it was too late. Jenna died and Reuben ran away. Jerusha was mad at Reuben, at the church, at me... but mostly at God. The doctor told me that if Jenna had come in when she first showed symptoms..."

"He works in mysterious ways," said Granny. "If Jenna had not died, you would not be here today, Jenny."

"That's true. But what happened with Eliza, Mandy?"

"The same thing. Levon's parents were Old Order, and they had raised Levon strictly. When they diagnosed Eliza, Levon followed the dictates of the church and brought in the Amish healer instead of taking her for more conventional treatment. By the time Levon got desperate enough to take her to an oncologist, she was stage four ovarian cancer. She only lived another six months. I don't think he ever forgave himself."

Bobby reached over and poured himself a little more coffee. "What happened then?"

"It devastated Levon, of course. He was at a complete loss. His parents were gone. He had no one to counsel him or help him through it. And Danny was distraught. He cried all the time."

Jenny clasped her hands together and bowed her head for a moment. When she looked up, there were tears running down her face.

Mandy touched her arm. "What is it Jenny?"

Jenny shook her head slowly. "Danny's story is so much my story. My birth papa died when I was only three in a terrible accident. Then my mama died a terrible death, and I was kidnapped and left all alone, lost in a storm. If they had taken Jenna to a doctor, I would still be lost, probably dead, long ago." She wiped her eyes. "I feel like *du lieber Gott* has placed me right in the middle of this. The only difference is that someone rescued me from my storm and Danny died. But I feel we are supposed to find the answer, Bobby and I together. It was Bobby and my papa who found Mama Jerusha and me in an abandoned cabin in the woods near Apple Creek. To keep us from freezing, Mama wrapped us in the Rose of Sharon quilt—the quilt my mama made in Jenna's memory. I still have the quilt. There are just so many similarities."

Bobby looked away and surreptitiously wiped his eyes. "I think the next step is to find Danny's father. That he should have completely disappeared is strange."

"Well, after Eliza died, the whole story got even stranger than you know."

"How is that?"

"Six months after Eliza died, Levon turned the management of the farm over to a cousin and got a job in Texas working with horses. He told us the name of the place, the Triple... something. I can't quite recall. He stopped by here on his way to Texas. He asked if Danny could stay with us for a while, but we were getting too old to handle a boy with Danny's problems. He understood and said he had another possibility—some distant cousins who lived in Colorado that had founded a Christian halfway house for troubled children. The Millers. He called them and they agreed to take Danny on a trial basis. After spending a few days here, Levon left for Texas. We only saw the two of them one more time. And that was the strange part."

Mandy went on. "When Levon left for Texas, I think he was trying to get away from all the memories of Eliza, so when he came through here, he had shaved his beard and was driving a truck. Definitely not Amish anymore."

Jenny was puzzled. "So, he left the Amish church, brought Danny here on his way to Texas, and wanted you and your husband to take him in?"

Mandy nodded. "Yes, but Mervin said no. We were just not able to take care of a boy with Danny's problems."

"And you never saw them again?"

"Actually, we saw them one more time. Levon showed up with Danny about a year later. He had a terrible time in Texas. He was in a house fire and he was terribly burned. His face was scarred, and he had grown his beard back to cover the scars. He was strangely different, especially in the way he treated Danny."

"How so?" Bobby asked.

"Danny had developed a severe anxiety disorder. He had persistent fears, worries or anxiety that disrupted his ability to take part in social situations. He was socially anxious and obsessive-compulsive. He always had his reader and Horse. They were his only friends. He was suspicious of everything and everyone else. Horse and the book were always with him. If anyone tried to take them, he would go almost catatonic."

"How did Levon treat Danny?" Jenny asked.

"It was as if he didn't care a bit about him. If Danny would cry, Levon would tell him to stop being a baby. He ignored him. And the strangest part was once when Danny and Mervin were alone together, Danny said 'not my papa.' It made my husband very suspicious."

Jenny looked at Mandy. "Were you suspicious, too?"

Mandy nodded. "Yes, but I didn't know Levon that well, and I just assumed he was still struggling with the effects of the fire and Eliza's death. Maybe Danny didn't recognize him because of the scars. Anyway, they were only here for one day and then they went back to Pennsylvania. Levon was going to sell the farm to his cousin and then go out west. He said he just couldn't bear the memories."

Bobby unconsciously reached for a Camel and then stopped. "What was the outcome?"

"Levon and Danny left. It was only a day later that the tree fell on Mervin and killed him. I never heard from Levon again. Oh, and there is one last thing. Mervin and I used to travel all over, going to quilting fairs and exhibitions... back when I was still quilting. I went to the Dalton Quilt Fair in 1992, the year before Eliza Died. It was the only time I went, but I don't remember meeting anyone named Roberta. As you know, Mervin and I were Old Order. The Bible tells us '*Thou shalt not make unto thee any graven image or any likeness of anything that is in heaven above, or that is in the earth beneath, or that is in the water under the earth.*' It's the second commandment. I never carried a picture of Danny."

11

THREE DEUCES

Jenny and Bobby sat at the kitchen table at the old Springer house in Apple Creek, talking about the case. They had organized all the information they could gather from Mandy and then driven back to Ohio. Granny had given them Jane Thompson's phone number at the Quilt Barn and Jane had agreed to act as a go-between if they needed more details from Amanda.

"Where do we go from here, Bobby?"

Bobby shook his head. "We have accomplished the main thing, and that is we know who our boy in blue denim is. Danny Wittmer."

"Did you say Danny Wittmer?"

Bobby and Jenny looked up. Daniel and Rachel stood in the kitchen's doorway, arms loaded with bags from the grocery store.

"Yes. The the murdered boy's name is Danny Wittmer, and he's from…"

"Smicksburg, Pennsylvania?"

Jenny looked at Daniel. "How did you know?"

"The Danny Wittmer I knew was the son of Levon and Eliza

Wittmer. Levon and his father owned a Morgan horse farm. The Wittmers bought their first Morgan from my papa."

Jenny shook her head. "This is amazing. So, you know Levon?"

"Levon Wittmer was one of my best friends. In my late teens, I was my papa's go between in business dealings with the Wittmers. We sold them the stallion, Black King, that got their Morgan business going and I visited there often. I was there the day after Levon met Eliza. I've heard of love at first sight and have even experienced it myself." He snuck a look at Rachel. "I'm not sure my wife has, though." He put on a face of mock sorrow and knelt at Rachel's feet. "My oh so distant, unapproachable Rachel."

Rachel punched Daniel in the arm. "That's mean, Daniel. You know I was a confused teenager. Everything I went through was because of my stubbornness. But I always loved you. I just couldn't admit it."

Daniel grinned. "So, the truth finally comes out. My wife is a stubborn girl who kept the boy who loved her from the first time he saw her twisting in the wind, and then made him come rescue her from horrible danger just to prove his love for her."

Rachel picked at a piece of lint on her sleeve. "That's pretty much it."

Bobby and Jenny, remembering the extremely difficult and dangerous times Rachel and Daniel had been through, both laughed.

"Anyway," said Daniel, "Levon loved Eliza from the first day he saw her. And she loved him." He set his bag of groceries down on the counter. "Does anybody know where Levon is?"

Jenny shook her head. "No one knows. He came back from Texas with Danny, stayed with the Beiers for one day, and then disappeared. Since then, no one has heard of him or his whereabouts."

There was a knock on the front door.

Daniel looked around. "I'll get it."

In a moment, Daniel was back with Detective Elbert Wainwright, who looked excited. "So, we know who he is?"

Jenny pointed to an empty chair. "Yes, we do, but as Alice said in Through the Looking Glass, 'Things are getting curiouser and curiouser.'"

"How so?"

"Well... here's what we know so far. Our boy is an Amish boy named Danny Wittmer. He was autistic. His father, Levon Wittmer, raised horses in Pennsylvania. Daniel knew Levon because their families both raised Morgan horses. Levon met an Indiana girl, Eliza Beier, in 1982. They were married in 1983. Eliza moved to Pennsylvania and Danny was born in 1984. When Danny was nine years old, Eliza contracted cancer and died. Levon, distraught over the death of his wife, left the church, shaved his beard, bought a truck, turned his farm over to some cousins and left for Texas. A year later, he was back. He stopped at the Beier's place in Shipshewana. Here's where it gets strange."

Rachel brought Elbert a cup of *kaffee*. He looked up and smiled. "Go on."

"It seems Levon was in a fire and it burned him badly. He had regrown his beard to cover the scars. He had Danny with him, but Danny's mental state had deteriorated. He told his grandfather that Levon wasn't his papa. To add to that, Levon did not seem to be the gentle man that the Beiers had met when he was courting Eliza. In fact, he was rough with Danny or ignored him. Mervin Beier, the grandfather, was suspicious. Levon stayed for one day and left with Danny. Only a day later, Mervin Beier died in an accident in the woods behind their house. He was alone. Amanda Beier never saw Levon or Danny again."

Elbert sipped his coffee. "Anything else?"

"Amanda, the grandmother, remembered part of the name of the ranch that Levon went to work on. It was near Amarillo, Texas, and it was 'Triple... something.'"

"How did the grandmother identify Danny?"

"From the picture."

Bobby spoke up. "And from the horse and the book that were with Danny when they found him."

Elbert nodded. "Ah, yes, the mysterious horse and book. Did she tell you anything about them?"

Jenny nodded and went on. "Eliza gave the book to Danny. She had it when she was a child. It was almost the only way Eliza could communicate with Danny. The horse, or 'Horse', as Danny named him, was Danny's constant companion. Amanda and Mervin gave the toy to Danny when he was four. And one last thing. Levon asked Amanda for a copy of Eliza's birth certificate, probably to help him in the farm's sale. He told Amanda that he lost all his papers, moving around. So that's where we are."

Elbert took a sip. "So, we know who the boy is, we know who the father is, but we don't know where Levon Wittmer is now?"

"That's about it," Bobby said. "And we don't know how Danny got to Indiana, and we don't know what part Roberta Kelly plays in all this. Oddly enough, Amanda does not remember meeting her at the Dalton Fair, nor ever showing anyone a picture of Danny."

Elbert looked at Jenny. "What do you think about all this, Jenny?"

"Well, it keeps coming back to me that things are not as they seem. There is a mystery within the mystery that needs unraveling. We have two options. We can end the investigation now and be happy that we have discovered who the boy is, or we can continue."

Bobby nodded. "By tracking down Levon Wittmer."

Jenny shook her head. "Yes, and that would mean finding the ranch he worked at and seeing if he left any clues behind that could show us where he went—or if anybody there has information that might lead us to him."

Elbert stared down into his cup, then looked up. "I think we need to keep going. And that means I'm going to have to call on you and Bobby for a little 'above and beyond' participation. I have some current cases on my desk that I need to focus on, that take me out of the loop for now, but I am definitely not satisfied that this case is even close to being closed. So, if I can keep you two on the payroll and turn you loose on the Texas angle, I would really appreciate it."

Bobby looked at Jenny, who nodded yes. "Okay Elbert, we're in. Couple of logistical questions. If we need to go to Texas, can you arrange the transportation?"

"No problem, Bobby. We have a pilot on the staff and the county has a Cessna Conquest that we use to travel to conventions and training sessions. I'm sure Brandon would love to get involved in an actual investigation instead of just flying detectives to parties in Kansas City."

"Okay, we are on it."

JENNY SAT AT HER OLD DESK IN HER WRITING ROOM ON THE SECOND floor. She had a phone book from Amarillo, Texas, open in front of her.

"Hmmm... let's see. Triple A, Triple Bases. Amy Tripple. James Tripple, C Triple... Triple Deuces..." Jenny paused. "Let's look at that one."

She opened the book to Triple Deuces. "Top Angus Breeders, Rodeo Horses, Racing Horses... this looks promising. 806-318-6077."

She picked up Bobby's cell phone and dialed the number. After three rings, someone picked up. "Triple Deuces Ranch, Slim speaking."

"Hello Slim, my name is Jenny Hershberger and I'm helping Detective Elbert Wainwright of the Wooster, Ohio police department with a cold case."

"A cold case?"

"Yes, that's a case that's been on the books for a long time, but has never been solved."

"Yeah, I know what a cold case is. How can I help you?"

"The case I'm working on involves someone who might have worked for you ten years ago, a man named Levon Wittmer."

There was silence on the other end of the line.

Jenny looked at the phone. She was still connected. "Hello? Hello, Slim?"

"Yeah, I'm still here. Did you say Levon Wittmer?"

"Yes. He would have worked for you in 1993 or 1994. Do you know him?"

There was another long pause. Then, "Yeah, I knew Levon."

"Did he work for you?"

"Listen, how do I know you're for real? Maybe you're working with the men that are after Levon."

"After Levon?"

"Yeah. How do I know you really work for the Wooster police department?"

"I can give you the number for Detective Wainwright. You can check it on the internet. Detective Elbert Wainwright. Just call him..."

"Why should I get involved in all this? That was a long time ago. Things happened back then that I'd just as soon not talk about."

"Please, Slim. This is very important. Have you heard of or read anything about The Boy In Blue Denim?"

"I think I saw something about that in the local newspaper."

"The boy is Danny Wittmer, Levon Wittmer's son. A local farmer found Danny, abandoned and dead in a snowstorm in Indiana ten years ago. We just discovered his connection to the Wittmer family. His grandmother is still alive and needs to have closure on this mess. One way we can do that is to find Levon. If you have anything you can share with us, please help us. By the way, my partner on this is Bobby Halverson, a retired sheriff. This is his phone. Have Elbert verify Bobby, too."

There was another long pause. "Okay, I'll check it out and if the numbers match, I'll call this Detective Wainwright."

"Then you'll call me back, right?"

"Okay, but I will not say a lot over the phone. There was stuff going on that could still put my life in jeopardy. If I get ahold of Wainwright and he verifies you, I'll call you back."

The line went dead.

<hr />

LATER THAT AFTERNOON, BOBBY AND JENNY WERE IN THE FRONT room when Bobby's phone rang. He answered it. "Bobby Halverson." There was a pause. "Yeah, Slim, she's right here."

Bobby handed Jenny the phone.

"Slim?"

"Yeah. I talked to Detective Wainwright and I guess you guys are on the up and up. I will say this. Yes, Levon Wittmer worked for me, but it didn't turn out well. He was a mess emotionally, and he got into some stuff that... well, took him down a hard road."

"What happened?"

"This is all I can say. He got involved with some bad guys. There was a shooting. Three men were killed, including a man who also worked for me and two big time cartel drug dealers. The house they were in caught fire and Levon was badly burned. I can't say anymore over the phone."

Jenny looked over at Bobby, then went on speaking. "If we come there, can you tell us more?"

Jenny heard Slim sigh. "Okay, but try to keep it as low key as you can. I don't want any uniformed cops or newspaper people here. Understand?"

Jenny nodded. "Okay, it's a deal. We'll fly down tomorrow. Can we reach you on this phone?"

"Fly into the Buffalo Airport. It's south of Amarillo, in Randall County. My ranch is close by. Call me tomorrow with your flight time and I'll meet you. Slim Watkins. I'll be wearing the Triple Deuces jacket and a white Stetson. Can't miss me, I weigh about two hundred eighty."

"Okay, we will see you tomorrow."

Jenny hung up. "We're going to Texas. Better call Elbert."

12

DEEP IN THE HEART OF TEXAS

Bobby and Jenny enjoyed an uneventful flight from the Wooster Airport to Amarillo. Brandon Williams, their experienced and personable pilot, was also a well-trained police academy graduate and licensed to carry. After a seven-hour flight, they landed at the Buffalo Airport. Brandon taxied the plane up to the small terminal. A large man with a white Stetson stood outside on the tarmac.

Bobby grinned. "Why do they always call the big guys 'Slim'?"

Brandon helped them with their travel bags. "I'm going to go file my flight report. Here's my cell phone number if you need me. There's a motel right next to the airport. Elbert booked three rooms. In the meantime, I'm going to get something to eat in the pilot's lounge."

Brandon strode away as the big man in the white Stetson walked up. He looked at Jenny with an amused expression as he held out his hand. "Slim Watkins. You must be Jenny and Sheriff Halverson." He shook hands with them. "So, an Amish detective. That's a new one on me. Don't see many Amish down here, much less Amish that are doing police work."

Jenny took her hand back and shook it.

Slim looked apologetic. "Sorry, Ma'am, didn't mean to crush you."

"I'm fine."

"These your bags?"

Bobby nodded. "We travel light."

"Did you bring a jacket? Sometimes Texas gets nippy in the fall."

Bobby pulled out a Camel. "We looked at the weather before we came, so we're good."

Slim looked around. "I thought we'd have dinner at my ranch. It's only a couple of miles and it's better to talk there. I'll feel more comfortable." He pointed to a large car parked at the side of the terminal.

Jenny looked at Bobby, who gave her a nod of acceptance. They walked with Slim to his car, a pretentious lime-green Mark IV Lincoln Continental. Slim opened the passenger door for Jenny and Bobby slid into the back. Slim climbed in and started the car. A Hank Williams song, 'Your Cheating Heart,' came out of the speakers. Slim nodded. "Around here there's only two kinds of music, Country and Western."

Slim drove through the airport gate and headed down the highway that ran past the terminal. The car was a smooth ride. Slim drove in silence. After about ten minutes, they turned off the highway under an over-spanning arch that read 'Three Deuces Ranch — Home of the best Broncs in Texas.'

"So Levon got on here because he was good with horses?"

Slim nodded as he pulled into a long circular driveway in front of a palatial house. "He was one of the best I'd ever hired."

Slim reached up and hit a button, and one of the garage doors opened. He drove in and the garage lit up. Checkerboard floors, immaculate shelving and one entire section was devoted to collector cars.

Bobby looked around. "Quite a collection, Slim."

Slim pointed to a bright yellow car. "That's my prize. A 1955 Ford Thunderbird, but not just a 1955, but the very first one off the line in 1954. It was Ford's answer to the Corvette. Come on inside."

The trio got out of the car and walked into the house through a large door. The place was indeed palatial. Slim led them through a couple of rooms into an immense dining room. A cheerful fire burned in the corner fireplace with a large table set for three in front of it.

"Hope y'all are hungry. We got steak and potatoes and some cherry pie for desert."

Bobby nodded. "Sounds like my kind of dinner."

"Can I offer you anything to drink?"

Bobby smiled. "A beer if you have one."

Slim called out. "Pete!"

A tall, older man with white hair and a short beard came into the room. "Whatta'ya need, Boss?"

"What do you like, Bobby?"

"Pabst Blue Ribbon is fine, but not many folks know about Pabst."

"Pete, bring Bobby a Pabst and for you, Jenny?"

"Some water with lemon will be fine."

Pete went out and returned in a few minutes with the Pabst and the water. "My dad was a Marine. The only beer he let in the house was Blue Ribbon."

"Did he fight in WWII?"

"Sure did, 1st Marine Division. Fought all the way through from Guadalcanal to the occupation of Japan."

Bobby smiled. "I was on Guadalcanal with the 2nd Marines and so was her dad." He nodded toward Jenny.

"An Amish man in the Marines?"

Jenny sat down at the table. "It's a long story, Slim. Maybe I can tell you sometime. But right now, I'm much more interested in what you know about Levon Wittmer."

"Right. That's why you're here. We'll chat over dinner. Bobby, sit there. Jenny, you stay where you are."

In a few minutes, Pete appeared with a couple of Hispanic-looking young men carrying trays loaded down with food. Hot platters with a huge steak, potatoes, asparagus, and sourdough bread.

Jenny saw Bobby's eyes light up. She shook her head. "I hope I can get a doggie bag."

Slim laughed. "Okay. You got it." He finished a bite and put down his fork. "Levon Wittmer."

Jenny looked over at Slim.

"Levon was a real enigma to me. When he arrived, I really liked him. He was polite, respectful, and an absolute whiz with horses. But…"

"But what?" Jenny asked.

"I guess you already know that Levon's wife died a few months before he came down here. It really devastated the young man. He just couldn't get past it. That's where Eli came in."

"Eli?"

"Eli Saunders. Eli worked for me. He grew up on a ranch in Fort Stockton and he knew horses. He came by several months before Levon got here, with a letter of recommendation from a friend out in west Texas, so I took him on. Eli was one of those hot shots. Always flashing a roll, although I didn't pay him that much. And he liked to throw his weight around. I had to get tough with him a few times when he got into it with some of the other hands. But he was exceptionally good with stock, so I gave more him more chances than I should have."

Jenny pushed her plate aside. "What did this Eli have to do with Levon?"

"What I didn't know about Eli was that he was running a side hustle."

Bobby pulled out a Camel. "Do you mind, Slim?"

"The smoking lamp is lit, Gyrene." Slim grinned.

Bobby lit up. "So, what was Eli's side hustle?"

Slim shook his head. "Drugs. He was selling to some of the young guys on the ranch and down at the stockyards. We sent him on the rodeo circuit with some of our broncs and he was selling there. I didn't find out about it until the trouble."

"How did Levon fit in?"

Slim got up and went to a table on the side of the room. He opened a humidor and took out a cigar. "I hope you don't mind, little lady?"

Jenny smiled. "I've been around Bobby too long. And my papa smoked when he came back from the war. It took him a long time to break the habit. Although Mama made him go sit on the porch." She giggled. "I think it was when she made him sit outside during a cold spell that he finally quit."

"So, like I said, Levon was extremely depressed when he got here. Oh, he did his work well enough. It seemed to take his mind off things, but when he was alone or off work, he would get way down in the dumps. Eli took advantage of him and got him strung out."

Jenny frowned. "You mean on drugs?"

"Yes. First pot and then smoking heroin. At least that is what I heard from some of Eli's inner circle. Levon could just shut the world and all his pain out with the drugs and so he did."

Bobby took a sip of his beer. "So, where can we find Eli?"

Slim shook his head. "He's dead."

Jenny turned toward Slim. "Dead? What happened?"

"Well, it seems Eli got in too deep with some drug cartel guys. They are all over the place down here. From what Levon told me in the hospital, Eli was at his house, which he also used for drug central. It seems he had a big deal going worth about $50,000. He got greedy and tried to rip off the cartel boys. There was a shootout between Eli and two of the drug guys. Levon showed up just as the fight came to a climax. Somebody fired a bullet through a propane tank on the back porch and the house blew up. Levon tried to go in help Eli but the explosion had killed Eli and the two Mexicans, and the flames burned Levon terribly. The drugs and the money went up in smoke. Levon ended up in the hospital. He was there for ten weeks. When he got out, he told me he was going to go get his son and go back to Pennsylvania."

Jenny leaned forward in her chair. "What exactly happened to Levon in the fire?"

"His face mostly. Scarred badly on the left side. He almost lost his eyesight, and he inhaled a lot of smoke and it scarred his throat. He sounded different after that. After his face healed, he grew a beard to conceal the scars. And his hands were burned."

Jenny reached into her bag and took out a manila envelope. She pulled out the picture of Danny. "Have you ever seen this boy?"

"Sure, that's Danny. Levon showed me his picture. He didn't bring the boy with him because Danny was too troubled and Levon had his own problems to work out. He left him in Colorado with a couple named Jerry and Sarah Miller. They were distant cousins who had a ranch in the San Luis Valley. It was like a Boys Town kinda place. Danny was there for the whole time Levon was here."

Bobby took out another smoke. "What did Levon say he was going to do when he left here?"

Slim shrugged. "He was going to get Danny, take him to Pennsylvania, sell the horse farm and head west. That's all I know."

Jenny got up and looked out the enormous picture window. A bright moon hung over the valley, lighting it up like daylight. "You said on the phone that there were things in this case that could put your life in jeopardy. What are they?"

Slim sighed. "There was $50,000 that the police never recovered. They assumed it burned up in the fire. But you must understand. The Cartel members are merciless. If they thought anybody got away with their money, they would track them to the ends of the earth. I don't want to stir this whole thing up again and maybe bring some of those ol' boys down on my head. I'm tough, but I'm not even in the same league with the Cartel."

"So, the Millers are in Colorado?"

"Yeah. San Luis is in the San Luis Valley. Beautiful spot. I heard there are even Amish there. Levon told me he was Amish all his life, but when his wife died, there were some things that happened that made him back away."

"You mean like not taking his wife to the oncologist, but relying on Amish healers?"

"That was a big part of it. Levon shared with me one night about all that. How he was so hung up on the rules and regulations that he couldn't see the forest for the trees."

Jenny took a deep breath. "This is all so sad."

Slim nodded. "Yeah, Levon was a messed-up guy when he came here, but when he left he... well, he changed. He was not the Levon I hired. I put it down to all the painful stuff he had been through, then the gunfight and his friend getting killed. They were pretty close, you know."

"Levon and Eli?"

"Yeah, we used to joke about it. They were a lot alike. Same height and weight. Eli was a little more outgoing, but when they were together, you might have mistaken them for brothers or maybe cousins. And they got along. Probably because Eli was making money off Levon, but they seemed to like each other."

Slim stood up and called out. "Pete?"

Pete stuck his head in. "Yeah, Boss?"

"Where's that cherry pie?"

The kitchen door opened and Pete came out with a deep-dish pie on a rolling tray. "Anybody that says they don't want some ice cream on this here pie better just head on down to Denny's for desert."

Bobby shook his head and nodded at Jenny. "You won't hear anything like that from the two of us."

13

A HORSE OF A DIFFERENT COLOR

Daniel King was sitting in front of the fire with Rachel in the Apple Creek house when a knock came on the door. Rachel went to open it and Daniel heard Rachel welcoming someone. "Why, Henry, come in."

It was Henry Lowenstein, their next-door neighbor.

Daniel looked up and smiled. "Come on in, Henry, sit down. Let the fire take the chill off."

Henry looked longingly at the comfy chair in front of the fireplace. "I'd love to, Daniel, but I need you to come over to the house. Bobby just called, and he wants to speak with you. He said he'd call back in fifteen minutes if I would bring you over. So here I am."

Daniel stood up. "Wonder what Jenny and Bobby have going on down there in Texas?" He went to the rack by the door and grabbed a jacket. "Rachel, why don't you put on some hot chocolate and I'll bring Henry back with me. And maybe heat up some of those cinnamon rolls you made. We'll sit in front of the fire and I'll update you on where your mom and Bobby are with the case after I talk with them."

Rachel headed for the kitchen. "Sounds perfect. See you both soon. Henry, mind you, come back now."

Henry grinned. "Yes, Miss Rachel. Indeed, I will."

———

Daniel and Henry went across the little bridge that separated the Springer house from the Lowenstein place. There was a definite nip in the air. The smell from the Springer fireplace drifted in the air, mixing with the smell of fallen leaves and creating an Ohio fall tang. They went up on the front porch of Henry's house and headed inside. After a five-minute wait, the phone rang. It was Bobby. Henry handed it to Daniel.

"Hey, Bobby, what's up?"

"Hi, Daniel. Well, as you know, we've been tracking Levon. We've been in Texas and now we are heading for Colorado. We are going to interview the folks who run the boys' ranch where Levon left Danny when he went to Texas."

"How can I help?"

Daniel heard the click of Bobby's old Zippo lighter and knew he had just fired up a Camel. He heard Bobby take a drag and then Bobby continued. "We talked to a man named Slim Watkins down here in Amarillo. Levon worked for him for a year. It seems Levon kind of went off the deep end during the time he was here. He got involved with a hotshot named Eli Saunders, who also worked at the ranch. Turns out Saunders was selling drugs."

Daniel pulled out a chair that was by the phone desk and sat down. "Go on."

"Slim said Eli got Levon into drugs, probably so he could make a customer out of him. Slim told us Levon was still deeply depressed over Eliza's death and his part in all that. So, the drugs became an escape for him."

Daniel shook his head. "Sorry to hear that."

"But here's the weird part. Eli got a little big for his britches and tried to rip off some drug cartel runners. Levon's story is that he showed up at Eli's house while a gunfight was going on. Just as he got there, someone fired a shot through the propane tank on the back porch and the place blew up. Levon tried to get Eli out, but it was too late. Eli and the two cartel boys were killed and Levon was burned badly on his face and arms."

"Wow, Bobby, that is weird."

"Slim said Levon was in the hospital for ten weeks. He let his beard grow back to conceal the scars once the burns healed, and then headed for Colorado to pick up Danny."

"So, what do you need from me?"

Daniel heard Bobby take another drag. "Slim said that Levon headed for Pennsylvania when he left Texas. He was going to sell the Wittmer farm and go west. Start a new life with Danny."

Daniel nodded. "Okay, so you want me to go to Smicksburg and see if all that happened?"

Bobby chuckled. "Great minds think alike, Daniel. Oh, and one last thing. Both Amanda and Slim said that after the fire, Levon was different. It wasn't his appearance so much. Except for the scars, he looked the same. It was the way he was toward them, and toward Danny. Different, rougher, less caring. Anyway, it seems like there's a lot deeper mystery here than just finding out who Danny Wittmer is."

Daniel stood up. "Okay, Bobby. I'll get in touch with Levon's cousins and Rachel and I will take a little train ride over to Smicksburg."

"Great Daniel. Keep track of your expenses and we'll get you reimbursed."

"Will do."

DANIEL AND RACHEL STEPPED DOWN ONTO THE PLATFORM AT THE Smicksburg train station. A burly, Amish man pushed through the crowd of arrivals and reached out his hand. "Daniel King. Haven't seen you for what, eleven years?"

"At least." Daniel turned to Rachel. "Rachel, this is Jeremiah Wittmer, Levon's cousin. I know him from back in the day when I was over here about once a month from Paradise."

Rachel smiled and extended her hand. "Nice to meet you, Jeremiah. I never met many of Daniel's childhood friends."

Daniel grimaced. "Not because I didn't try."

Rachel punched Daniel lightly on the arm. "Never gonna let me live that down, are you, blondie?"

Jeremiah grinned. "It's okay. We know all about you, Rachel. Big boy here spilled his guts about the only girl in the world every time he came—" He ducked as Daniel lunged toward him and beat a hasty retreat. "Whoa, okay, okay. Where are your bags? You're staying out at the farm. Beryl is cooking a big dinner. Jonathan and Noah are coming. It will be just like old times... Except Levon won't be there."

<hr>

DANIEL PUSHED BACK FROM THE TABLE, HOLDING HIS STOMACH. "Goodness, Beryl, what a feast."

Beryl blushed. "It's the least I can do for such an old friend."

Rachel stood and picked up some plates. "Let me help you with the cleanup, Beryl. I know these fellows need to talk."

Beryl smiled. "Most appreciated. When they are done, we will warm up the fresh cherry pie and pour the *kaffee*."

The two women began cleaning off the table, while Jeremiah motioned for Daniel and the other two cousins to come into the sitting room. Jeremiah began. "So, you are here to ask about Levon?"

Daniel nodded. "I don't think they have released the information yet, so I'm telling you this in confidence. Have any of you heard about The Boy In Blue Denim?"

Noah nodded. "I work at the mill and some guys were talking about it."

"Did you see any pictures of the boy?"

The cousins shook their heads. "We are Old Order, so we rarely read newspapers and never watch television," said Jeremiah.

Daniel took a deep breath. "The little boy was Danny."

There was a moment of shocked silence around the room. Finally, Jonathan spoke. "Our Danny? Danny Wittmer?"

Daniel nodded. "Yes, I'm sorry to say. My mother-in-law, Jenny Hershberger, got some information down at the local Paradise newspaper. She writes a column about the Amish for them. When the article about the mysterious boy in blue denim came out about a month ago, a woman sent her a letter identifying Amanda Beier as Danny's grandmother."

Jonathan drew a breath. "Eliza's mother."

"Yes. So Jenny and Bobby Halverson, a retired ex-sheriff, and a long-time family friend, went out to Shipshewana and found Amanda. When she saw pictures of Danny and other information, Amanda confirmed that the boy, who has been a John Doe in a grave in Indiana for the last ten years, was Danny Wittmer."

Jeremiah sighed. "Oh, my. This is terrible. *Wie konnte das passieren?*"

Daniel shook his head. "This is what we are all trying to find out. I got involved because, of course, I knew Levon and all of you. Strange how all this tied together." Daniel looked over at Jeremiah. "Can you tell me about the last time you saw Levon?"

"It was 1994," said Noah. "He came here with Danny. He was... I don't know, different."

"How?"

"The scars, I guess. That was the most obvious. His voice was unfamiliar, too, but he said he had breathed in flames when he was in the house fire and it burned his vocal chords. But most of all..."

"He was very nervous," broke in Jonathan. "He wasn't the easy-going Levon we knew. He was here to sell us the farm and get out as quick as he could. He could have asked much more, but he said he wanted to make it easy so it would happen quickly."

"Of course, we asked him if this was what he wanted," said Jeremiah. "After all, he and his papa had built this farm from nothing. But he was adamant. And he would get a bit...cranky, I guess, if we hesitated or just wanted to make sure."

"What about Danny?"

Jonathan spoke. "When Danny was here with us, when Eliza was still alive, Levon was a wonderful papa. He and Eliza could not have loved the boy more. Despite Danny's problems, they cared for him with such tenderness. They loved him deeply. But..."

"But what?"

"When Levon brought him here after he came from Texas, it was as though he couldn't care less about Danny. When we asked him about it, he got *sehr ängstlich*, you know, defensive. He tried to explain to us he still had not recovered from Eliza's death and his part in it."

Daniel nodded. "Do you mean because he would not take Eliza to a cancer doctor?"

"Yes," said Jonathan. "He seemed very troubled and deeply into his own problems, so much so that it seemed caring for Danny was only an afterthought."

"So, you bought the farm from Levon?"

"Yes. He had all the papers, everything was in order. He stayed in the area, long enough for the property to go through escrow, and then he left. We got a good price, but the whole negotiation and sale was very strained."

Daniel sighed. "So Levon comes back from Texas a different man; nervous, distracted, defensive and not very caring toward his son."

"That's about the size of it," said Jonathan.

"Yes," said Noah, "the woman with Levon seemed much more caring than Levon."

Daniel sat up. "Woman?"

Jonathan nodded. "Yes, he had a woman with him. He never said if they were married or not, but they seemed to be a couple. She tried to keep Danny calm, and he seemed to relate to her better than to any of us."

"What was her name?"

Jonathan looked over at Jeremiah. "Do you remember?"

Jeremiah thought for a moment. "Levon called her Bobbie. Wait a minute." Jeremiah got up and left the room. In a few minutes, he was back. He had some documents. "These are some papers we had to have notarized. Levon had her sign as a witness. She had to produce identification." He handed the documents to Daniel. Below the signature of Levon was another, in a feminine hand.

Roberta Kelley.

14

THE MILLERS

"San Luis Valley Regional Airport right below us." Brandon picked up the radio handset. "San Luis Regional Tower, Cessna Conquest 8121K 10 southwest at 2,500, inbound for landing with Sierra."

The radio crackled. "Cessna Conquest 8121K, San Luis Regional Tower, report entering left downwind Runway 1."

Brandon answered. "Report entering left downwind, Cessna Conquest 8121K. Cessna Conquest 8121K entering left downwind runway 1."

Another crackle. "Cessna Conquest 8121K, cleared to land Runway 1."

Brandon answered, "Cleared to land Runway 1, Cessna Conquest 8121K." He slipped the handset back into its holder on the dashboard. "Okay, down in ten minutes."

JENNY AND BOBBY STEPPED OUT OF THE PLANE. BRANDON LEANED out of the window. "I'm going to gas her up and hang out here. I checked the map and San Luis is about ten miles. Do you have the address?"

Bobby nodded. "Yes, and I think we have a ride." They picked up their bags and walked toward the terminal. There was a sheriff's department cruiser parked in front of the terminal and a tall and lanky bearded man in a sheriff's uniform leaning on it. He stood up when he saw Bobby and Jenny. "Sheriff Halverson?"

Bobby nodded. "Yes, and this is Jenny Hershberger."

The Sheriff stuck out his hand. "John Lane, Alamosa County Sheriff. I don't know if you remember, Sheriff, but we met at the National Sheriff's Association Conference in DC about ten years ago. You were being given a lifetime award."

Bobby looked closer. "Sure, John Lane, only you didn't have a beard then."

Sheriff Lane grinned. "And I was a lot wetter behind the ears. I'm surprised you remember me."

Bobby tilted his head toward Jenny. "That's one reason she keeps me around, Sheriff. I still have a sharp memory for names and faces. And yes, I remember you well. That was a very special time for me. I was a sheriff for thirty years and I met some great people, many of whom were at that convention. You were a deputy then and your sheriff was Jim... Jim..."

"Jackson."

"Right. How is Jim?"

"He's retired, has a ranch over by Jürgen Hirschberg's place in San Luis. They raise Mustang horses together. Jürgen is Amish, like you, Jenny."

"Have there always been Amish here?"

Sheriff Lane nodded. "For a long time. Jürgen's father came here from Germany in 1940. He brought his Jewish wife. They escaped Germany when the Nazis marched into the Rhineland. The Hirschberg's story is pretty amazing."

Jenny smiled. "Hirschberg comes from the same root as Hershberger. It's a mountain in Switzerland. A lot of Amish came to America from there." The historian in Jenny lifted its head. "If I had time, I'd love to chat with them."

"Maybe we can arrange it. In the meantime, where do you need to go? I got a call from Detective Wainwright and I'm at your disposal."

"Appreciate your help, Sheriff. We need to visit an organization outside of San Luis, The Good Shepherd Ranch. From what we understand, it's like a Boys Town."

Sheriff John nodded. "I know the place well. Perry Miller runs it."

Jenny was putting her bag in the car, but she stopped and turned to the sheriff. "I thought Jerry and Sarah Miller ran it."

The sheriff shook his head. "Another mystery of the wild west. Jerry and Sarah were there one day and gone the next. They just vanished."

Bobby looked at Jenny. "And when did that happen, Sheriff?"

"Well, let me see... I'd say about eleven years ago. Fall of 1994."

PERRY MILLER GOT UP FROM BEHIND HIS DESK AND GREETED THE interesting trio entering his office. John Lane, he knew. A very diverse couple accompanied John—a fit-looking old man with white hair and a baseball cap with a sheriff's association badge, and a still lovely Amish woman, probably in her mid-sixties.

Sheriff Lane introduced Bobby and Jenny.

Perry motioned to some chairs. "Please, make yourselves comfortable. John, always good to see you. How can I help you folks?"

Jenny started. "We are here to find out about Danny Wittmer and his father, Levon."

Perry stiffened and turned toward Jenny. "Did you say Levon Wittmer?"

Jenny noted Perry's reaction. "Yes, do you remember him?"

Perry nodded, took a deep breath, and looked out the window. "Yes, I remember Levon Wittmer very well. He enrolled his son Danny here in 1993. I remember him because he returned for Danny a year later and it was the day after they left my folks disappeared."

Sheriff Lane spoke up. "Like I said, it's one of the unsolved mysteries of the San Luis Valley."

Jenny glanced at Bobby. "Cold cases seem to follow Bobby and I around. A farmer in Indiana found Danny Wittmer suffocated in a snowstorm over ten years ago. That would be about a year after Levon came and picked him up. They buried him as a John Doe, and it was only last week that we established his identity. Now we are trying to put everything together. We need to find Levon Wittmer."

Perry shook his head. "So, Danny's dead, too."

"Too?"

Perry went on. "My folks are dead. I know that without a doubt. They were the most responsible parents, and they loved this place. They never would have gone off and just vanished. Something terrible happened to them and I'm pretty sure Levon Wittmer had something to do with it."

Bobby shifted in his chair. "Why do you say that?"

"I was 20 when Levon Wittmer brought Danny to Good Shepherd. Danny was troubled. We knew little about autism back then; very few kids had it. But when we had our resident doctor examine him, Danny showed all the classic signs. Withdrawn, unfocused, uncommunicative. He had his horse and his book and they were his only friends. His dad tried to reach Danny, but he had his own troubles. His wife had just died, and it had impacted him deeply. He begged my mom and dad to take Danny, at least until he could get back on his feet. They only agreed because he was a cousin."

"We've been told that he had rejected the Amish faith. Is that true?" Jenny asked.

Perry nodded. "My dad told me Levon grew up Old Order Amish, so I was expecting the whole Amish thing. But he was beardless, wearing western clothes and driving a truck. I guess he had moved away from the church. At least it appeared so."

Bobby spoke up. "So why do you say that Levon had something to do with your folk's disappearance?"

"It wasn't so much what he did when he first came here, it was when he came back for Danny that I got a very odd feeling about him."

"Like what?"

"He was different. Oh, he looked the same, except his beard was back—he had been in a fire or something and he had ugly scars on his face." He thought for a moment. "No, it wasn't so much the physical appearance that was different. He looked the same. It was the way he treated Danny. He tried to pretend he was concerned about Danny, but he didn't act like a dad. The woman that was with him was much nicer to the boy."

Jenny perked up. "Woman?"

"Yes. Her name was Bobbie."

Jenny felt an excitement rise inside her. "Bobbie? Did she give a last name?"

"Kerry, or Keely... no Kelley, Bobbie Kelley."

Jenny looked over at Bobby. "The mysterious Roberta Kelley re-enters the story."

Bobby nodded.

"Re-enters?" Perry asked.

"We got into this case because a few weeks ago I received a letter from a Roberta Kelley telling me she had seen an article on Danny and she knew who the grandmother of the boy was. When we went to the address on the letter, the house was empty and abandoned. A neighbor told us someone named Bobbie lived there years before with a man, a very mean man. To top it all off, Amanda says she can't remember meeting Roberta at the Dalton Quilt Fair and she certainly did not show anyone a picture of

Danny. Now a Bobbie Kelley shows up with Levon in Colorado. This is all strange."

"Not any stranger than my parents disappearing just after Levon Wittmer left."

Bobby looked over at Sheriff Lane. "When the Millers disappeared, what was the protocol? Did the department do a full-out search?"

Sheriff Lane nodded. "We scoured the area. I think maybe Perry should fill in the details of why we didn't continue searching for longer than a week."

Perry started up from his chair. "I don't see—"

"It's been ten years, Perry. I know you don't want to disparage your parents' memory, but I think you should tell Sheriff Halverson and Jenny."

Perry dropped back in his chair, his shoulder sagging. "All right. It seems my mother had been doing some juggling with the scrip fundraising program. I don't think she really meant to commit a crime. She just got short in her accounts and was about to face a serious investigation. It would have meant ruin for the ranch. When the details came out after they vanished, the police felt that Mom and Dad left rather than face a public shaming. I think the idea is preposterous. My dad was the most honest man I knew. My mom was a little scatter-brained, kind of an old hippie at heart, but they would have worked it out. And they never would have gone without telling me. No, something very bad happened to them."

Jenny spoke up. "Sheriff, when you searched, was it only in the valley?"

"Yes. We didn't have a reason to go elsewhere. It seemed like a cut-and-dried case. Couple leave to avoid a scandal. And I had little to say about it. Sheriff Jackson was in charge and he was very close friends with Jerry. I think he felt it was better to just let it all die down. He probably thought they just need time to think it through. I don't think he even reported them missing. But they never came back."

"How about in the next state? Did you look in New Mexico?"

"No, I doubt it. We're pretty rural down here, and the national databases were pretty antiquated back then."

Bobby stepped in. "Do you think it might be worthwhile to do a missing persons request in New Mexico, focus on the next counties over the line? Maybe they have some information that might be helpful."

"I don't suppose it would hurt. I'll do that today. Will you be around?"

"We'll stay in town until you hear."

<hr>

Jenny was in her room in the motel in Alamosa when there was a knock on the door. "Who is it?"

"It's Bobby."

Jenny opened the door and Bobby came in. "Sheriff Lane just got a call back from the Taos police department. It's an hour south." He paused. "They have two unclaimed bodies that were discovered by hikers about five years ago in a rugged canyon up Wheeler Peak. They were both shot in the head. They have the skulls and part of the bodies, and they are sending them over for dental comparisons."

"It's them, Bobby, it's the Millers. I just know it. And Levon Wittmer and Roberta Kelley are right in the middle of it."

15

ROBERTA

J enny, Bobby, and Daniel sat with Elbert Wainwright in his office. Elbert was thumbing through their reports while the others sat quietly. Finally, he put them down.

"It seems we have opened a real can of worms here. When I started all this, I just thought we might find out who the murdered boy was. Now we have three unsolved murders and a formerly mellow Amish man who's turned from Doctor Jekyll to Mr. Hyde. I wonder..."

"Wonder what, Elbert?" asked Jenny.

"Didn't you say that Mervin Beier died mysteriously right after Levon Wittmer showed up from Texas?"

Jenny nodded. "Yes, and that was right after the Millers disappeared."

"Did you get a forensics report on the bodies they found in New Mexico?"

"Yes, we did. It was the Millers. Somebody shot them both in the back of the head, execution style. The forensics lab said they had been dead around ten years."

"Which puts the murders right around the time they disappeared," said Bobby.

"And something else," said Jenny. "When the police realized it was the Millers, they sent out search and recover parties. They found the Miller's car at the bottom of the most inaccessible canyon on Wheeler Mountain. So, Levon must have driven them up the mountain, killed them and then abandoned their car where the police wouldn't find it."

"Which means," said Bobby, "that someone else followed Levon up there to pick him up after he did it."

"Roberta Kelley."

<hr>

ELBERT LOOKED AROUND. "SO, WHENEVER LEVON WITTMER SHOWS up, somebody dies. How long after Levon left Shipshewana, did Mervin Beier die?"

Jenny looked at her notes. "Amanda said it was only a day after Levon and Danny left."

"Very interesting trail of unexplained deaths."

"And Roberta Kelley is right in the middle," Jenny agreed, "but..." She thought for a moment. "Amanda didn't mention her being with Levon and Danny."

Daniel spoke up. "Maybe Levon didn't want to let the Beiers see her. After all, it had only been a year since Eliza's death. Maybe he didn't want to let them know he had moved on from their daughter. It would certainly have made them suspicious of him."

Bobby nodded. "So, he kept Roberta back at the motel while he saw what he could get from the Beiers."

"Yes, Eliza's birth certificate," said Jenny.

Elbert shuffled the papers and then looked up. "I think we need a new plan of action. I'll outline one and you all add anything that you feel we need. First, we must find Levon Wittmer. Of equal importance is locating Roberta Kelley."

Jenny looked over at Elbert. "Yes. Roberta addressed her letter from her old house in Centerville, but the postmark was from Stroudsburg. So perhaps we can contact the Stroudsburg police department. She may be in their database."

Elbert glanced at a report. "We have an excellent description of her, from Perry Miller and the Wittmer boys." He shook his head. "You know, I don't think she's the sharpest knife in the drawer. If she wants to get even with Levon by outing him, why did she use her real name?"

Jenny smiled. "You know, most criminals are not very smart. At least the ones who get caught. They always make a foolish mistake."

Elbert went on. "So, we have to find out where Levon and Roberta are now. And we have to figure out why Danny was in Indiana."

"Plus, we need to account for the year between when Levon picked up Danny from the Millers and when they found him in that shed," Bobby put in.

"Daniel, any ideas?"

"I'm not sure. But I am wondering if this Levon that brought Danny to Shipshewana is legitimate. His behavior sure doesn't sound like the Levon I knew." Daniel's face lit up. "How about if I go back to Smicksburg and get copies of the contracts that Levon signed to sell the farm? My father still has paperwork from Levon and his papa that they signed when we bought or sold horses. Levon signed many of those. We could compare signatures. And if I could meet with him in person, I could ask him one question that would tell me if he's the real deal or not."

"Great idea, Daniel," agreed Elbert.

Jenny spoke up. "What puzzles me is why Roberta, who seemed to be Levon's companion, would reveal the whereabouts of Danny's grandparents."

Bobby shook his head. "From all I've heard, the Levon that came back from Texas was a mean guy. Maybe Roberta was just tired of his rough ways, or he hurt her badly. Hell hath no fury..."

Elbert interjected. "Bobby, we need to find Roberta Kelley right away. If she's so mad at Levon, maybe she'll give him up. Stroudsburg, did you say, Jenny?"

"Yes, that's where the postmark was from. Roberta has something to hide, but she also has some sort of connection to Danny. Both Perry Miller and the Wittmer cousins noticed she seemed to really care for Danny. Why else would she get involved in all this? And why did she say she met Amanda at the Dalton Fair, even though Amanda says she never met a Roberta? I think she somehow knows about my past and used the Quilting Fair to make sure I would get involved. She's gone to a lot of trouble to expose Levon Wittmer." Jenny frowned. "I think I told you all that right from the beginning I've gotten the feeling that things are not as they seem. Appearances can deceive, and I don't think we are even close to figuring out the genuine mystery behind this story." She looked around. "Roberta was probably with Levon in Texas because she showed up in Colorado and then in Smicksburg. So, she wasn't just an innocent bystander. She is deeply involved in this mystery." Jenny went quiet for a moment, then looked around. "You know, I have a hunch. And if I am right, it will tie all this together. So, while you and Bobby go over to Pennsylvania to find Roberta, I think Daniel and I need to make another trip to Texas."

<hr>

Elbert and Bobby sat in the waiting room outside Police Chief Waylon Allgood's office. They were in Stroudsburg, Pennsylvania. They had not been waiting long when the door opened and a small man with a narrow mustache and a baseball hat with Police Chief embroidered on it stepped through the door. "Sheriff Halverson?"

"Retired sheriff."

The chief grinned. "Show me a cop who's retired and I'll show you a dead man." He turned to Elbert. "Detective Wainwright, I presume. Waylon Allgood."

Elbert nodded and stuck out his hand. "That's me."

The Chief nodded toward his office. "Come on in, fellas. Can I get you some coffee?"

Elbert and Bobby both nodded affirmatively.

"BETTY!"

"Coffee, Chief?" came a voice from down the hall.

The chief looked at his visitors. "Cream?"

Bobby nodded.

"YEAH, WITH CREAM, BETTY!"

"On the way."

The three men retreated into the office. Chief Allgood motioned them to two chairs in front of his desk. As they settled in, he went around to his side of the desk and sat down. There was a folder and some newspapers in front of him. He shuffled through them.

"Well, Detective, I've been going through your files and I even got copies of the local newspaper from a month ago when they ran the article on The Boy In Blue Denim. Quite an interesting case." The Chief patted them into a coherent pile and looked up. "Now, what's my part in all this?"

Elbert shifted in his chair. "Roberta Kelley."

"Roberta Kelley?"

"Yes, the mysterious Roberta Kelley. The Amish woman we are working with, Jenny Hershberger, got a letter from someone named Roberta Kelley. In that letter, Kelley gave Jenny a clue as to the whereabouts of a person she claimed was the grandmother of dead boy, a woman named Amanda Beier. Kelley supposedly met her at a quilting fair in Ohio that figured in Jenny's own life. We traced Amanda Beier to Shipshewana, Indiana, and established the boy was a ten-year-old Pennsylvania lad named Danny Wittmer and that Amanda Beier was indeed the grandmother of Danny Wittmer. We also confirmed his father was Levon

Wittmer, the Beiers deceased daughter's husband. We traced Wittmer from Smicksburg, Pennsylvania, to Shipshewana, Indiana, and then to Amarillo, Texas. From there, the trail led to Colorado, back to Shipshewana, and then back to Smicksburg. All along that trail, we have been finding dead bodies."

There was a knock on the door and a stout, older woman came in with a tray loaded with coffee cups. "Here's the coffee, Chief."

Chief Allgood nodded toward a table by the wall, and Betty set the tray down. She passed out coffee and when she lifted the cream, Bobby nodded.

Chief Allgood smiled. "Thanks, Betty." Betty nodded and then left. The Chief turned back to Elbert. "Go on with your story. It's quite interesting."

Elbert took a sip and then continued. "In Texas, Wittmer got involved with a drug dealer named Eli Saunders. Saunders was killed when a propane tank exploded during a gunfight with some drug traffickers and Wittmer was badly burned in the fire that resulted from the explosion. Wittmer left Texas, picked up his son at a boy's ranch in Colorado where he had been staying, returned for a day to Shipshewana to see the grandparents, showed up in Smicksburg to sell his horse farm, and then disappeared. A year later, they found Danny dead in the snow in Indiana. As Bobby and Jenny pushed their investigation, a woman named Roberta Kelley surfaced in the company of Levon Wittmer —after he left Texas, and in Colorado. She was also with him in Smicksburg. We think it's the woman who wrote the letter."

"So, what brings you here?"

"The letter Jenny got from Roberta had a Centerville address on it, but the letter had a Stroudsburg postmark. So, we came here to see if we could get any information about her."

"So how did this Amish woman, Jenny Hershberger, get involved in all this?" asked the Chief.

Bobby spoke up. "Jenny Hershberger is a historian and a writer who knows more about the Amish communities of Pennsylvania, Ohio and Indiana than probably anyone living. She and I worked with Elbert on a case over in Wooster last year that involved a long-hidden murder in the Amish community."

The Chief nodded. "The girl in the box. I read about that."

Bobby smiled. "That's Jenny."

Elbert chimed in. "We couldn't have solved the case without her."

"I've known Jenny almost all her life," said Bobby, "and interestingly enough, she and I sat in this very office over forty years ago with a retired detective named Bill Martin. We were looking for Jenny's birth mother. And we found her mother right here in this building—at least her belongings."

"Bill Martin. Yes, his picture's out on the wall in the hallway. I'd like to hear that story."

Elbert smiled. "We will have to have Jenny come over. She's a real pistol. One of the sharpest minds I've ever met."

Chief Allgood took a sip of his coffee. "So, you need our help in finding Roberta Kelley?"

Bobby nodded. "If we could look through your database, you know, for any crimes, DUI, Petit theft, anything that would put her on your radar. Also, if you could get us in to the Tax Assessor's office, we might find her through tax records. She is at least a material witness and possible an accessory in several murders—Danny Wittmer, Jerry and Sarah Miller and perhaps Mervin Beier."

The chief got up and went to the door. "BETTY!"

Down the hall came a plaintive voice. "You have an intercom, Chief." They heard Betty's chair scrape as she got up. "Be right there."

In a moment, Betty came in. The chief handed her the folder of material. "These fellows are to have full access to all our records. They need your help with the queries they need to run in the system."

"Sure thing, Chief. When do you want to get started?"

Elbert stood up. "As soon as possible."

Betty smiled. "Come right on down to my office, then. If Roberta Kelley is in Stroudsburg, we will find her."

Chief Allgood grinned. "That intercom is good for a lot of things, eh Betty? Like listening in on my private meetings?"

Betty blushed. "I'm still trying to figure it out, Chief. I must have pressed the wrong button."

ELBERT WAINWRIGHT STOOD IN THE SHADOW CAST BY A LARGE ELM tree on a back street of Stroudsburg. He watched while the Stroudsburg police silently slipped around the side of the older white Cape Cod-style house. The chief stood next to him and Bobby was just behind them. The chief's walkie-talkie clicked. "In place, Chief. All exits covered."

Chief Allgood nodded to Elbert, and they walked up to the front door of the house. He knocked and then called out. "Police. We have a warrant. Open up!"

There was quiet for a moment and then suddenly there was a crash of broken glass from the back of the house.

Someone on the other side of the house yelled. "Police! Stop right there!"

The three men heard a woman cry out. "Leave me alone. I ain't done nothing."

A cry came from the back yard. "Got her, Chief."

Chief Allgood, Elbert, and Bobby hustled around to the back of the house. Stark lights lit up the backyard. In the middle, a woman struggled with three officers. Chief Allgood stepped up. "If you don't want us to put you down on the ground and hogtie you, then stop struggling."

The woman looked around and then stopped.

"Roberta Kelley?"

She nodded. "Yes, what of it?"

The chief looked serious. "Roberta Kelley, I am arresting you as an accessory to the murder of Danny Wittmer and Jerry and Sarah Miller. You have the right..."

"I don't know no Levon Wittmer."

Roberta Kelley sat in Chief Allgood's office in an orange jail jumpsuit, glaring at the chief. Elbert and Bobby stood quietly against the wall as Allgood interrogated her.

"Wittmer. Well, Ms. Kelley, unfortunately we have at least four people who can identify you as being in the company of Levon Wittmer at different times. We also have witnesses who can identify you as being seen with Danny Wittmer before someone killed him."

Roberta paled and then opened and shut her mouth. She reminded Elbert of a catfish gasping for breath after someone pulled her out of a river.

The chief went on. "Ms. Kelley, you can either be a hostile witness or you can cooperate. Either way, we are going to extradite you back to Ohio for now, where Detective Wainwright is investigating you on some very serious charges." He looked down at the paper in front of him. "Accessory to murder before and after the fact, kidnapping, fraud, and, if we can tie you directly to the deaths of Danny Wittmer and Jerry and Sarah Miller, first degree murder. I believe that Ohio, Indiana, and Colorado are capital punishment states. So, wherever you end up in this convoluted case, if the investigators and the prosecutors do their job, you could take a permanent trip out of this world. If you cooperate, we take that into account."

Roberta Kelley gulped and looked around. "I… I don't know no Levon Wittmer."

"That's your story and you're sticking to it, eh? Well, don't say I didn't offer you the chance to get on the right side of the law." He leaned over and clicked the button on the intercom. "Betty?"

"YES, CHIEF!" echoed down the hall.

Allgood pushed the button again. "Intercom, Betty."

There was a click and Betty came on. Elbert could almost see her blushing. "Yes, Chief. I'm still not used to you using this thing. What do you need?"

"Please send in Sergeant Ferrell to take our prisoner back to her cell. And did Detective Wainwright give you those extradition requests?"

"I'll send him right in and, yes, I have the papers. We are just waiting for the governor's warrant from Ohio."

"How long does that take?"

There was a pause, then Betty came on. "Only a week and a half. Detective Wainwright filed an 'expedite' request. And the Ohio Governor's Office said that the governor has taken quite an interest in this case."

Just then, a burly sergeant came through the door. He motioned to Roberta. "Off we go."

Roberta stood and turned to go.

The chief glanced up. "I'm going to give you one more chance to come clean, Ms. Kelley. Otherwise, you'll go back to face a trial for the murder of a little boy with no credits on your side. If this goes to trial, it will be hard to find a jury that isn't secretly prejudiced against you. What say you?"

Robert scowled at the men in the room. "I ain't saying nothin'. And I want to see my lawyer."

"All right, Ms. Kelley. Have it your way."

Jenny and Daniel sat with Slim Watkins and Detective Roland Watkins from the Wooster Police Department in the Randall County Sheriff's Office. It was a blustery Texas day outside. Elbert had assigned Detective Watkins to accompany them to Texas to help with their business. The door opened and the sheriff came in.

"Howdy folks. I'm Sheriff Tim Jackson. Welcome to Amarillo; at least our half of Amarillo." He smiled. "Most folks don't know, but Amarillo forks the county line between Potter County and Randall. So, Amarillo has two sheriffs. We're the southern boys and we try to cause them Yankees in Potter County as much trouble as we can. Slim, good to see you."

"Tim, been awhile."

His visitors relaxed.

"Now, what can I do for you?"

Slim looked at Jenny. "Do you want me to lay it out?"

Jenny nodded. "Thank you, Slim."

Slim began. "First, this is Jenny Hershberger, Daniel King, and Detective Roland Watkins. Detective Watkins is here as the liaison between you and the Wooster, Ohio, Police Department, and the Ohio Governor's Office. Jenny and Daniel are outside investigators who are working with Wooster on this case. Let me explain. Ten years ago, there was a shoot-out at a house in south Amarillo. Three men died. One of them was Eli Saunders, who had worked for me as a steer salesman and a horse wrangler. The other two were Sinaloa Cartel members who were picking up fifty thousand that Eli Saunders was supposed to deliver from the sale of their drugs."

"Yes, I remember that. Wasn't there someone else involved?"

Slim nodded. "Yes, a man named Levon Wittmer who also

worked for me. He was a client and a friend of Saunders and he arrived at the house just as a gunfight was breaking out. Saunders had told him what he was going to do and Wittmer was there to talk him out of it. But he was too late. A bullet struck a propane tank, and the house exploded, killing Saunders and the other two men. Wittmer was terribly burned, and the fire incinerated the other three."

"And you are privy to the inside information because...?"

Slim looked at Jenny and went on. "Levon told me what happened when I went to see him in the hospital."

The sheriff frowned. "I remember that case. We had some details, but not as many as you have, Slim. We just thought it was some local boys fighting over drug territory. I didn't know Sinaloa was involved. We got some information from Wittmer at the hospital, but not what you just told me. I didn't see you at the inquest. This information would have been most helpful."

Slim looked down. "I didn't want to get implicated, Tim. There was fifty thousand of the cartel's money that burnt up with Eli, and I didn't want those people to connect me to the case. Like I told Jenny, I'm a tough guy, but the cartel boys make me look like Elmer Fudd."

The sheriff turned to Jenny and Daniel. "What's your involvement in this?"

"I got the letter that started us on the trail to Shipshewana," Jenny said, "and put us on the trail of Levon Wittmer. It concerned a boy they found murdered in a snowstorm ten years ago. No one knew who he was, so they dubbed him The Boy In Blue Denim. Perhaps you have heard about him?"

"Yes, I have."

"The letter I received helped us identify the boy as Danny Wittmer, Levon Wittmer's son. And there is a tie-in that grabbed my attention right away."

"And what was that?"

"When I was three years old, a man who killed my mother

with a drug overdose kidnapped me. He headed out to California, but he drove into the Thanksgiving super storm of 1950 in Ohio. He crashed his car in Jepson's pond just outside of Apple Creek, Ohio. The woman who became my stepmother was on her way to the Quilt Fair in Dalton, just up the road. Her driver crashed the car and went for help, but he never came back. She left the car to get to an abandoned cabin in the woods where there was wood and a fireplace. On the way, she found me. So a woman who was going to the Quilt Fair saved me in a snowstorm. When I got the letter, the woman said she met Levon Wittmer's mother-in-law at that same Quilt Fair. Danny was a little boy who died in a snow-storm. There were just to many parallels, so I contacted Elbert, Detective Wainwright—"

"My boss," interjected Roland.

"Yes," Jenny went on. "We had worked with Detective Wain-wright on another case involving the Amish community, so he asked us to get involved in this one."

"And Daniel?"

"Daniel is my son-in-law, but he's also very involved in the case. He and Levon Wittmer were best friends and their families worked together in the horse business for years. He can identify Wittmer when and if we find him."

"So, what do you need from me?"

Jenny looked at Roland, who picked up the thread. "We just received word from my boss that the Stroudsburg police picked up the woman who wrote the letter to Jenny. My office and the governor are working to get her extradited to Ohio. She's charged as an accessory in the murder of Danny Wittmer and a couple named Jerry and Sarah Miller of San Luis, Colorado. We believe that Levon Wittmer was responsible for the deaths. We believe the person who passed himself off as Levon Wittmer ten years ago may not be Levon Wittmer at all. We need to establish Levon Wittmer's identity, so we are here with a request to disinter the three bodies... the remains of the three bodies... of the men who died in that fire ten years ago, so we can do DNA testing."

Sheriff Tim nodded. "I think we can arrange that."

JENNY, DANIEL, AND ROLAND WATCHED AS THE EXCAVATOR SCOOPED away the dirt above the graves. They had buried the three men in a pauper's field. Only one grave had a notation—Eli Saunders.

Sheriff Tim watched as the crew lifted the boxes from the graves. "I feel like I dropped the ball on this one. Wittmer was not a friendly witness. He had been badly burned and was mostly out of it on pain killers. He said Saunders got into a fight over drugs with some dealers and just as he arrived, the house blew up. Se we just assumed it was Saunders and two unknowns. We never checked identities past that."

Jenny looked up at the sheriff. "Sometimes things are not what they appear to be. That thought has been coming back to me throughout this investigation. When we started, we were just trying to find out who Danny was. Now we are deep into three murders and a drug deal gone wrong."

"What's the next step, Sheriff?" Roland asked.

"We turn the bodies over to forensics and then they establish the DNA. After that we need to find someone whose DNA matches the established sample."

"So, if one of the dead guys is actually Levon Wittmer, then DNA from his cousins should be a close enough match to establish that?"

"I would think so. If they are cousins the DNA would show a common ancestor only two generations away."

A cold fall wind whipped through the graveyard. Jenny took Daniel's hand. "I hate to say this, but I hope it is Levon. I just don't want the gentle man that married Eliza to turn out to be a cold-blooded killer."

17

───────

MERVIN

"The whole incident was strange. I never knew Mervin to be a careless man."

"Tell us what you mean, *Bischof* Lehman."

Jenny, Daniel, and Roland were sitting in the front room of the Lehman farm in Shipshewana. They had come there from Amarillo with Roland to find out more about Mervin Beier's death.

The old man stood and went to the window. Outside, the immaculate lawn rolled down to the road. A line of elm trees marched along the lane, the few remaining leaves clinging to their remembrance of summer. Fruit trees stood in a small orchard to the side of the house, and the spectacular red barn set off the entire setting.

"Well, Mervin was a very meticulous man. Everything in order, everything in its place. When he was doing a project like the one that killed him, he always was very methodical. First step first, second step next, you know, a perfectionist."

Jenny took a sip of the tea that the *bischof's* wife had brought in. "So what exactly happened?"

131

"We found Mervin crushed under a tree that he had been pulling down with his team. The police assumed that something had startled the team, and they jumped ahead before Mervin was ready. But I was very skeptical of that report."

"Why, *Bischof*?"

"Mervin Beier had the best trained team of horses in LaGrange County. He won many competitions with them. I never saw them move a step without Mervin's command. They stood like rocks, even if a dog barked or a gun went off. He trained them from colts and they were a wonderful team. The best I ever saw."

"So, who found Mervin?" Daniel inquired.

The *bischof* turned. "Some boys who were playing in the woods found him. He was under the tree and the horses were just standing there in harness. They were Amish boys, so they came to me first."

Roland spoke up. "Was there a coroner's report?"

The *bischof* nodded. "Yes, but we were not privy to it when he drew it up. We heard it read at the inquest. They ruled it accidental, but I have always had doubts."

"Because of the horses?" Jenny asked.

"Yes, exactly."

Roland stood. "I think we need to go down to the coroner's office and see his files. I called Elbert from Texas and he FedExed the release documents ahead of time."

THE LAGRANGE COUNTY CORONER, GEORGE FRANKLIN, WAS AN older man with a gray fringe of hair around a bald spot on the top of his head. He was genial and accommodating.

"Yes, Mervin Beier, I remember that case. Accidental death. Something spooked his horses, and they jumped while Mervin was under the tree."

Jenny hesitated, then went ahead with her question. "Did you know that the Amish *bischof* always had doubts about your ruling in that case?"

Franklin looked surprised. "No, he never said a thing. Of course, they keep to themselves, the Amish..." He smiled at Jenny and Daniel. "No offense meant, ma'am."

Jenny smiled. "None taken. It's very true, Mr. Franklin."

"What were his concerns?"

Daniel spoke. "The *bischof* told us that Mervin's horses were perfectly trained. They never moved unless Mervin commanded them. So, he found it difficult to understand why the team would shy and pull the tree down, especially since they would have to do a continuous pull to get the tree out. He is right. I've trained horses all my life. A team that is pulling down a tree must pull and pull hard for several minutes, even if the roots are dug out. Someone has to be directing them, even if they are not trained to stand."

Franklin took out a note pad and wrote something down. "So, you are saying that it is very unlikely that Mervin would have been caught under that tree... unless..."

Jenny nodded. "Unless he was already unconscious and placed there."

The coroner stood. "Perhaps we should look at my records. Follow me, please."

The trio followed Franklin down a hall and into a large room lined with filing cabinets. Franklin went to a cabinet, opened it, and leafed through. "Here it is." He went to a table on one side of the room and motioned them to come.

"These are the photographs taken at the scene and my photographs of the body once they delivered it here. The Amish objected to an autopsy, but Indiana law requires one in all cases of questionable death." He spread out some pictures on the table.

"This one is how they found Mr. Beier." The photo showed an

older man face down on the ground with a large tree on top of him. The tangle of branches growing off the main trunk held the man down.

Jenny pointed. "So, did the tree crush his body? Is that what killed him?"

The coroner shook his head. "No, it appeared that a large branch struck him on the head. That's what killed him. The limbs you see here were spread out around the body, trapping it, but not crushing it. My ruling was one of those large secondary branches struck his head on the way down."

Roland picked up the picture. "Can we see the ones of Mervin after they brought in the body?"

"Yes, but..." he looked at Jenny... "they are gruesome."

"It's all right, Mr. Franklin. I need to know."

The coroner pulled out some pictures. They were from several angles. Mervin Beier's head was severely injured. There were at least two places where the skull was crushed in and covered with heavy blood flow.

Daniel pointed to the main indentation in the skull. "I don't want to tell you about your business, but it seems like these were not made by a blow from one of the limbs that was holding Mervin down. Those branches were all around the head, but not directly in contact. Wouldn't a limb heavy enough to kill him have crushed the whole side of the head?"

The Coroner looked closer. "I believe you are right, Mr. King. In my assumption as to the nature of the case, I missed this. Those indentations look like something smaller than a large branch made them..."

"Like a hammer?" asked Jenny.

The corner nodded. "Definitely."

Jenny took hold of Daniel's arm. "I think we need to go out to Amanda Beier's and look through the wagon Mervin had out at the site. One must have been there with a saw and splitting tools."

Daniel nodded. "Right, and he unhooked the horses and hitched them to a pull chain. The wagon would have been right there."

"In here." Amanda Beier opened the door to the barn. Light came in through the large door and spotlighted a heavy wagon standing in the middle of the open space.

Roland put on some gloves. "Let me handle this, so it's official and we maintain chain of custody on anything we find. Where would the tools be, Amanda?"

Amanda pointed. "In that box on the side of the wagon. Just lift the lid."

Roland approached and lifted the lid, fastening it up with a hook and eye on the side of the wagon. He lifted out tools one by one. "Ah, this is interesting." He lifted out a metal ball peen hammer. Holding it up in the light, he examined it. "There appear to be some reddish stains on the ball." He looked at Amanda. "And no one has touched these tools since they brought the wagon home?"

Amanda shook her head. "No. I just put it in the barn and closed the doors. It's been in here ever since."

Roland slipped the hammer into a plastic bag, sealed it, and put a date and location information on a tag attached to it. "We'll take this to the sheriff and have it dusted for prints and tested for blood. There is a very good chance this is the weapon the killer used."

Amanda gasped. "Killer! Are you saying that my Mervin didn't die from an accident?"

"It's very possible, ma'am. We are going to check it out."

"Levon!"

"What about him, ma'am?"

"There was something very wrong about Levon Wittmer when he came here with Danny. He was mean, rough, distant. He said he needed Eliza's birth certificate so he could sell the farm. Mervin was very suspicious, especially after Danny said 'not my papa.' In fact, Mervin kind of hinted to Levon that he didn't believe his story about the fire and his injuries. It made Levon furious. He grabbed Danny and stormed out of here. We never saw him again."

Jenny took Amanda's hand. "All I ever bring you is bad news. I'm sorry."

Amanda slipped her arm around Jenny's shoulder. "No, no, Jenny. *Der liebende Gott hat dich zu mir gebracht, um mir zu helfen, die Wahrheit zu erkennen.*"

Jenny nodded. "Yes, He is the truth, and He wants us to know the truth, even if it hurts at first."

Daniel spoke. "What was it Bobby suggested? When Levon was last here, he left Roberta in a motel so that Amanda wouldn't be upset?"

Amanda looked puzzled. "Roberta? Who is Roberta?"

"She is the woman I told you about, the one who sent me the letter that opened up this entire case. She was with Levon in Colorado and in Smicksburg. Which probably means she was with Levon when last he came here."

"We could check the records of the local motels and see if they stayed here... when would that have been, Amanda?"

"Mervin died in the fall of 1994, September 27."

"How many motels and hotels are in town?"

"There is only one worth mentioning, The Blue Gate. Back then, there were not very many. The Amish craze had not infected the *Englischers* yet." She smiled. "Let me see, Blue Gate, Farmstead Hotel, Morton House and The Van Buren."

"Shouldn't be too hard to check. Most of the motels keep records for a long time," said Roland. "Let's go make some inquiries."

ROLAND BROUGHT THE EVIDENCE BAG TO THE SHERIFF IN LaGrange. "I believe there are bloodstains and there may be prints. The hammer is metal, and it has been undisturbed since Mervin's death, so there may be latent prints as well. It's been ten years, so be very careful. "

The sheriff took the bag. "You got it, Detective. I have the best forensics team in the state. If there is anything here, we'll find it."

"Coroner Franklin has the blood samples from Mervin Beier. If you find anything, he can make a match. If there is blood on the hammer, it will most likely be Mervin's."

"Anything else you need?"

"Yes. We have made some inquiries at some local hotels to see whether Levon Wittmer stayed there in or around September 27, 1994. They all said it will take a few days. I told them to send the results of their search to you. If you would be so kind to put all your findings in a report and forward it to my boss, Detective Elbert Wainwright in Wooster, Ohio, that would be much appreciated."

"I'll expedite it."

"Oh and, by the way, did I tell you that this case is very much tied into the case of The Boy In Blue Denim?"

"Really? How?"

"Mervin Beier was the grandfather of Danny Wittmer. That's the boy's name. And the person we are looking for as a person of interest in the murder of Mervin Beier is Danny's father, Levon Wittmer."

"Wow! The Boy In Blue Denim case has been a blot on LaGrange County for ten years. Jimmy Clark was the sheriff back then and when he retired, his biggest regret was that he never found out who the boy was. I'll call him and let him know what you folks are onto. And George Franklin, the coroner, worked on that case. He was the one who discovered that someone suffocated the boy—that he didn't freeze to death in the storm."

Roland took off his hat and scratched his head. "Boy, what goes around comes around, doesn't it?"

"Sure does. I'll let George know. He'll take extra care."

18

———

THE NET TIGHTENS

Jenny sat with Bobby and Elbert in the break room at the Wooster Police Station. Elbert took a bite of the sandwich he was working on, chewed reflectively for a moment, then wiped his lips with a napkin. "So, what are we waiting on, Jenny?"

Jenny looked at her notes. "We are waiting for the DNA tests from the three bodies in Texas, the forensics report to see if there were any bloodstains and fingerprints on the hammer in Mervin's wagon, the motel records from Shipshewana to find out if Levon and Roberta were still in Shipshewana when Mervin died, and signature comparisons from the Wittmer boys real estate sale and Daniel's father's earlier horse sales."

"And if none of it matches up...?"

"We're up the creek without a paddle," scowled Bobby.

Jenny agreed. "If none of it turns out as we suspect, then all we have is the identity of The Boy In Blue Denim, which is enough. It answers the first question we all had. But I have a deep sense that *Gott* has taken us everywhere we needed to go and given us everything we need to solve this mystery."

"And remember, we also have Roberta Kelley. Pennsylvania

signed the extradition, and she will be on her way here within a week."

"May I have permission to talk to her when she comes?"

"If she agrees, Jenny. Otherwise it can't happen."

Jenny sighed. "I have to speak with her. She's the key to everything."

Elbert agreed. "I'll do my best Jenny. In the meantime, I put out an APB on Levon Wittmer. It's gone out on the police network for crimes of foremost priority and dangerous suspects. If Wittmer is still in the United States, we should be able to pick up his trail."

THE FIRST SNOW OF THE YEAR HAD COME EARLY TO APPLE CREEK. A week before Thanksgiving, Central Ohio received a half-inch dusting. Jenny and Rachel took a walk in the old neighborhood. The temperature had dropped below freezing and the two women bundled up. The snow made everything clean and fresh and Jenny tried to let it lift her spirits, but something troubled her and Rachel could tell.

"What's wrong, Mama?"

Jenny thought for a few moments without speaking. Then she took Rachel's hand. "Oh Rachel, I just feel that I'm missing something very important."

"But, Mama. You tracked down Roberta Kelley, you found out the identity of The Boy In Blue Denim, you've thrown a great deal of light on this whole terrible mess. Just to find out that the boy is Danny Wittmer is a huge win."

Jenny nodded. "Yes... I know Rachel. But something keeps bothering me, and I don't know what it is. I keep going back to those pictures of Papa and me when we were running away. The people in those pictures were not who they seemed to be. Papa looked like a hippie and I looked like some little band groupie."

Rachel giggled. "Mama, how did you find out about groupies?"

Jenny smiled. "I read a lot, Rachel, and it's not confined to Amish history. Your papa told me some stories about when he lived in the Haight Ashbury, and even when he was a famous Christian song writer and producer after we lost him for those eight years."

"When he had amnesia and thought he was somebody else."

"Yes, and that's my point. We keep thinking people in this adventure are somebody they are not. And I feel very stupid because there is something right in front of me and I'm missing it."

"Maybe if you get to talk to Roberta, you'll find what you're looking for."

Jenny took her daughter by the arm as they walked. "That's exactly what I'm hoping, Rachel... exactly what I'm hoping."

Jenny sat at the conference room table and looked over the forensic reports from LaGrange County. George Franklin had signed them and he included a note thanking Jenny and Bobby for pursuing the Wittmer case. His report was very straight-forward.

In examining the metal hammer found in Mervin Beier's tool kit, I found that the reddish stains were indeed blood specimens. Our lab extracted DNA from the sample and compared it with DNA from blood samples taken during the autopsy of Mervin Frederick Beier in September, 1994. We stored the sample under Barcode # 10262577.

Summary of Analytical Procedures;

1. *Differential Extraction of evidence samples*

2. *Microscopic examination for the presence of cells and the confirmation of human blood*
3. *QIAGEN BioRobot EZ1 magnetic bead-based DNA purification*
4. *Quantitative PCR using the Quantifiler Duo kit*
5. *Amplification of the Identifiler Plus STR loci using the Polymerase Chain Reaction*
6. *Capillary electrophoresis and analysis of ampliefied DNA*

Results:

See attached table 1 for DNA testing results

Conclusions:

The samples were a match to 99%. The DNA in the blood on the hammer was a 99% positive match to the samples taken from Mervin Beier in 1994 and preserved as autopsy evidence. The portion of the hammer with the bloodstains was a match to the three fracture indentations in the top of Beier's skull. We also found two clear fingerprints in the blood residue, both of which bore scarring, but were intact enough to use for identification. The fingerprints did not match those on Mervin Beier's gun registration card. Our conclusion is that the person who wielded the hammer that struck the killing blows left their prints in the blood residue.

The Coroner's Office hereby reverses its initial verdict of accidental death to murder by person or persons unknown.

George Franklin — LaGrange County Coroner

JENNY LOOKED UP. "THERE IT IS. MERVIN WAS MURDERED."

Elbert handed Jenny another report. It was from the Van Buren Hotel in Shipshewana. It was a confirmation that Levon Wittmer, Roberta Kelley and a child had occupied Room 227 for three days—from September 25 to September 27, 1994, checking out in the late afternoon of the 27th. There was a guest register and credit card receipt attached to the report. Levon Wittmer signed the register.

Jenny looked at Bobby. "The net is closing on Levon Wittmer."

THREE DAYS BEFORE THANKSGIVING, BOBBY RECEIVED A CALL FROM Elbert.

"We got him, Bobby."

"Levon?"

"Yep. Found him in Wyoming on a farm outside Casper."

"How did they get him?"

"Somebody who was looking for him tracked him down. There was a shootout. A couple of sheriff's deputies were driving by and got the drop on the shooters. They saved Levon and arrested the men. Turns out they were cartel members. Those guys never give up. I think we will find that it goes clear back to Texas."

"So, what about Levon?"

"They took Levon into town and called in a report to the U.S. Marshals Pacific Southwest Regional Fugitive Task Force. These are the guys who locate and apprehend the most dangerous fugitives and assist in high-profile investigations."

Bobby grinned. "So, what exactly happened?"

"The Task Force checked for any outstanding warrants. They found my APB. They tipped off the sheriff, and they arrested Levon on the spot. As soon as we can get the Ohio governor to sign another warrant, we will start the extradition process. He should be back here by Christmas."

"Doesn't sound like it will be a merry Christmas for Levon and Roberta. Thanks for calling, Elbert. I'm gonna go break the news to Jenny."

JENNY, BOBBY, DANNY, AND RACHEL SAT AT THE TABLE IN THE Springer house in Apple Creek. Jenny took a sip of *kaffee.* "What shall we do for Thanksgiving?"

Rachel shrugged. "Well, I don't think we can go home to Paradise for the holiday. There's too much happening here. You want to be here when the Marshals bring Levon and Roberta here. Daniel needs to be here, too. Besides, your grandkids are watching both houses and doing a great job. Daniel's father has the horse farm well in hand, and your cousin has buttoned up everything for the winter in Paradise, so..."

"What about Rusty?" asked Bobby, plaintively.

Rachel smiled. "From what I hear from the kids, he's doing fine. They take him out every day. The walks are very healthy for him."

Bobby patted his stomach. "I should probably be there to walk with him. We're coming up on Thanksgiving and just thinking about it makes me gain weight."

Jenny put her cup down. "I agree with Rachel. Levon Wittmer and Roberta Kelley will be back in Apple Creek soon. We want to see this through."

Daniel chimed in. "How about an old-fashioned Springer house Thanksgiving?"

Jenny looked at Daniel. "You remember my mama's feasts?"

Daniel shook his head. "Unfortunately, I was never there. But Rachel told me all about them. Let's see; there was turkey, fresh rolls, dressing, corn, squash, carrots, yams, green bean casserole..."

Rachel chimed in. "...Pumpkin pie, apple pie, cakes, brownies and cookies..."

Bobby rubbed his chin. "My mouth is watering. I remember Jerusha's cooking. She was the best. I was here many times. Your papa and I would bring in wood for the fireplace, while Jerusha made the feast. And then when you got old enough, Jenny, you pitched right in."

"I needed my mama's guiding hand, though. Not only could I not quilt, I was a terrible cook in those days. I was just too 'buzzy' to settle down and learn how to do it. When we lived here after Jonathan disappeared, I settled enough to learn a few things."

Rachel patted Jenny's arm. "Whatever you were then, Mama, you certainly improved."

Jenny smiled. "Yes, if I set my mind to something, I go after it until I make it my own."

Bobby looked around. Everyone was grinning. "Jenny Hershberger, that may be the overstatement of the year."

Jenny stood up. "All right. Apple Creek thanksgiving it is. Rachel, why don't you run over and invite Henry. And, Bobby, you call Elbert. It's about time he got a taste of the inner workings of the Amish life."

Daniel stood. "Make a list, Jenny, and Bobby and I will run to the store. If I'm right, if there is going to be enough, we'll have to start cooking yesterday."

INSIDE THE NIGHT CLUB, THE MUSIC CHANGED FROM LOUD TO SOFT. Gentle chords drifted sweetly out the door as a lyric saxophone danced a sweet melody above them. And then a beautiful, clear voice lifted over the chords, and words that she never thought to hear again broke upon her senses.

Tonight, I whisper in your ear,
I always want you near.
Tonight, kiss me tenderly,
Come so easily,
Into my heart, tonight.

Jenny's breath caught in her throat.

A lover's symphony,

The sweetest harmony,
And all that I can be
Is here with you tonight
I'll do the best I can
To be your loving man,
And everything I am
Is here with you tonight.

With each line she heard, a deeper shock pierced Jenny's heart. She turned and stared at the door.

"That song…"

In a trance, Jenny moved through the door and back into the club. It took a moment for Jenny's eyes to adjust. The bright stage lights were almost blinding, and she could barely make out someone sitting at the piano, singing a song.

Tonight I sing this song of love,
You're the one I'm dreaming of tonight.
Kiss me tenderly,
Come so easily,
Into my heart tonight.

As the band picked up the melody, Jenny walked slowly through the club. She didn't see the people. She only saw a man sitting at the piano—a man with shoulder-length dark hair and sunglasses. She couldn't see his face because he was turned away from her as he played. She kept moving forward until she stood directly behind him. His clear voice lifted, like an angel singing…

A lover's symphony,
The sweetest harmony,
And all I want to be
Is here with you tonight.
I'll do the best I can
To be your loving man,
And everything I am
Is here with you tonight.

The words...Jonathan's words...it was the song he wrote for her. She stood in wonder as the man came to the last verse. And then she lifted her voice and sang with him, for she knew the song by heart.

Tonight, I sing this song of love.

You're the one I'm dreaming of.

Tonight, kiss me tenderly,

Come so easily

Into my heart tonight.

As the band played the last chords and stopped, the man slowly turned. The lights glared off the sunglasses and Jenny still couldn't see his face. She spoke.

"Where did you get that song?"

The man turned his head to the voice. "I wrote it."

"No, you did not. My late husband, Jonathan, wrote it."

The man recoiled as though someone had slapped him. "Jonathan?"

Jenny moved closer. "Who are you?"

"I'm...I'm Richard...Richard Sandbridge. I wrote...I wrote..."

Jenny reached up and gently removed the sunglasses. The face...so familiar, but different. The mustache...the...oh, Lord! The eyes! The eyes...the wonderful sea-blue eyes, just like her papa's. The eyes that drew her in and in until she was one with him.

"Jonathan? Jonathan?"

The man looked puzzled. "No, I'm...I'm Richard...Who are you?"

"Jonathan, it's *me*. It's your Jenny."

Richard reached out, his hand shaking. "Jenny?"

Jenny took her hair and rolled it up into a bun. She grabbed a pin out of her purse to hold it. Then she lifted out her *kappe* and put it on.

"Jonathan, it's your Jenny. It's me."

He stared at her, and then the light of recognition broke upon his face. Both of his hands reached out. Jenny took them in hers. The old shock ran up her arms and into her heart.

"Jenny! Where have you been? It was so dark...oh, Jenny..."

Jonathan moved off the bench and stood before her. Jenny reached out and touched his face, gently, oh so gently, and then she was in his arms and he was holding her and his powerful arms were around her and...

"Oh, Jonathan! Jonathan!"

And then the man held Jenny at arm's length and looked her full in the face. "You see, Jenny? Things are not what they seem. You thought I was dead. I wasn't. I thought I was Richard Sandbridge, but I was Jonathan, your Jonathan. Keep going, Jenny, keep searching. Follow this road to the end..."

And Jenny woke up

19

QUESTIONS AND ANSWERS

Jenny sat in front of her mirror, brushing out her silvering hair. The few locks of remaining bright red had softened to a subtle auburn. She remembered the picture taken at the roadside stand, almost fifty years before, with her wild red curls popping up in a pixie cut and Jonathan's hair down his back.

And then she remembered the dream from the night before... such a dream. She had dreamed about the night she found Jonathan alive after he had been missing for eight years. He was performing at a concert, singing the song he wrote for her, an amnesia victim who had built a whole new life as a Christian producer and record company owner. *Du lieber Gott* led her to him by a long and convoluted series of incidents, including the tragic death of her parents.

The dream was so real.

It surprised her to find tears starting.

I miss Jonathan so much. It's been ten years. It's fresh every day. What did he tell me in the dream?

She thought for a moment and then it came to her.

He looked me right in the eyes and said; You see Jenny? Things are not what they seem. Follow this road to the end...

I'll try. Gott, gib mir Weisheit und Offenbarungswissen.

There was a knock on the door.

"Yes?"

"It's me, Mama."

"Come in, Rachel."

The door opened and Rachel came in. Jenny turned and looked at her beautiful daughter. Her red hair tempered by Jonathan's black, Jonathan's sea-blue eyes with just a hint of the violet that suffused hers. Her face; so much of Jonathan's extremely good looks in her daughter's face. Suddenly, without knowing why, Jenny put her hands to her face and burst into tears.

Rachel moved to her and knelt beside her. "Mama? What's wrong?"

Jenny put her arms around Rachel and pulled her close. "I dreamt about your papa last night, about the night Bobby and I found him at the nightclub. I came there to meet Jeremy, but I heard Jonathan singing while I was outside."

"Oh, Mama."

"It was so real, Rachel. He was Richard Sandbridge. He was singing the song that he wrote for me years before. It was one of the few things he remembered through the amnesia. He didn't know me. I had to put on my *kappe* and then I saw his eyes change. He knew me." Jenny pulled Rachel closer.

"Oh, Rachel, I miss your papa every day."

Rachel stroked Jenny's hair tenderly and let her mama sob against her breast. When Jenny finished, Rachel pulled a hanky from her pocket and handed it to her mama.

"Your papa told me again that things are not as they seem. When he was Richard Sandbridge, I thought he was dead. I lived like he was dead. I almost fell in love again, but he was alive all that time. And when that train accident injured my mama and papa so terribly and I was with them at the hospital..." Jenny wiped her eyes and blew her nose.

"When my papa died, the machine he was hooked to kept recording a pulse. And then I realized it was because my mama was holding his hand. Mama's heartbeat was being picked up on papa's machine. It was like they had one heart. And then I knew Jonathan was the only man I would ever love, that he and I shared one heart. And then he came back to me and if Gott had not showed me that things were not as they seemed…"

"You might have married Jeremy and never seen Papa again."

Jenny nodded. "And that's how this mystery is. Levon Wittmer is not what he seems. Roberta is not what she seems. And unless we get down to the truth, we will miss the real meaning of all that we have found. And with *Gottes hilfe* we will find the answer that's been hidden for so many years."

Rachel smiled. "I know you will solve this, Mama."

Rachel paused and then looked at Jenny. "Now, 'why did Rachel come to get me,' you're thinking."

Jenny looked at her daughter blankly.

Rachel giggled. "The turkey, Mama. The turkey."

"Oh," gasped Jenny. "The turkey. We have to get the turkey in the oven."

Rachel nodded. "Yes, Mama, unless we want sushi turkey."

Jenny shook her head. "No sushi turkey for me. Give me two minutes to dress and I'll be right out. Did you take it out of the freezer?"

"Several days ago, Mama."

"You're such a good girl, Rachel. I am so blessed to have you."

Rachel blushed and then went to the door. "Bobby and Daniel are sitting in the kitchen waiting for dinner."

"Tell those big lugs to get the stove fired up and to get started on the whipping cream and the ice cream. Put them to work and give them some samples along the way."

JENNY SAT ALONE AT HER DESK. IT WAS LATE IN THE DAY ON Thanksgiving. Everything had gone wonderfully. Bobby, Daniel, Rachel, and Elbert were sitting in the front room in front of a fire finishing some *kaffee*. Outside it was snowing again and the white flakes waltzed by the window. Jenny laughed to herself.

Elbert's eyes had almost popped out of his head when he walked in the door and saw the table loaded with food. "If this is how the Amish eat, it may force me to reconsider my denominational preference."

Now Jenny was recording the facts she had gathered.

Danny is the Boy In Blue Denim. His father was Levon and his mother was Eliza. Danny had autism.

1993. After Eliza died, Levon went to Texas. On his way, he stopped in Shipshewana and met with Mervin and Amanda Beier. He then dropped Danny off with Jerry and Sarah Miller at The Good Shepherd Boy's Ranch in San Luis, Colorado. Danny was there for a year while Levon worked for Slim Watkins at the Triple Deuces Ranch outside Amarillo, Texas.

Late 1993. Levon met Eli Saunders, a drug dealer. Saunders got Levon, who was in a very depressed state following the death of Eliza, addicted to drugs, pot, and heroin.

1994. Then Saunders was reportedly killed by an explosion during a shootout with drug dealers. The resulting fire in the house where the gun battle took place burned Levon terribly. Levon was in the hospital for ten weeks, then he left to go back to Pennsylvania to sell his farm.

1994. Levon stops in San Luis to get Danny. Roberta Kelley is with him. The day Levon leaves with Danny, the Millers disappear. Hikers discover two bodies in a rugged canyon in New Mexico five years later. The bodies remain unidentified until 2005 when we contacted the police in New Mexico. After they identify the Millers, they find the Miller's car in a steep canyon not far away from where they found the bodies.

1994. Levon returns to Shipshewana. Danny is with him. He has changed drastically, both in appearance and behavior. After Levon allegedly leaves, Mervin Beier dies in an accident. In 2005, after visiting Amanda Beier, Bobby, Roland Watkins, and I recover a metal ball peen hammer that proves to have bloodstains and an excellent set of prints on the head and handle. The coroner changes Mervin's accidental death verdict to murder by person or persons unknown. Hotel records show that Levon and Roberta remained in Shipshewana during the time-period when Mervin died.

1994. Levon returns to Smicksburg and sells the farm. Danny and Roberta are with him. Levon's trail ends here. Danny disappears until someone murders him in Indiana. Roberta Kelley disappears.

1995. They found Danny Wittmer dead in a snowstorm in rural Indiana.

2005. Jenny receives a letter from Roberta Kelley detailing a meeting with Danny's grandmother, and the investigation begins.

2005. Police apprehend Roberta Kelley in Stroudsburg, Pennsylvania. Sheriff's deputies arrest Levon Wittmer in Casper, Wyoming. Both are under extradition orders and are to return to Wooster in December.

"Jenny?"

It was Bobby.

"In my office, Bobby."

Bobby Halverson came into the room. He looked very satisfied. "Just want to tell you, that was a splendid dinner. It was good to be here at thanksgiving. Brought back a lot of memories. Jerusha, Reuben, all of us together; especially Reuben."

"So, you think of Papa, Uncle Bobby?"

Bobby sank down in a padded chair by the wall. "There isn't a day goes by that I don't remember your dad. Did I ever tell you how we met?"

Jenny grinned. "Something about a fight in a bar?"

Bobby looked out the window at the falling snow. "The first time I met Reuben, I was drinking in my favorite bar in Wooster. It was November 1941. I usually drank alone. I usually sat at a small table in the back of the room where it was dark and I could nurse a brew while I watched the goings-on without having to put up with some stupid drunk trying to make conversation. At a table near the bar, a bunch of construction workers had been going hot and heavy for a while and were getting noisier and more obnoxious with each pitcher of beer. One man, a big red-faced loudmouth named Clancy, was doing the lion's share of the talking..."

"I tell you, we're going to get into it with the Japs pretty soon," he said thickly, "and when we do, we'll show 'em what it means to mess with Americans. If we go to war, I'm signing up on the first day. What about you?"

"I got a wife and kids," mumbled another worker named Smitty. "I'm not so sure I want to get all shot up, so I'm no good to my family."

"What are you, yellow?" Clancy snarled. "Nothin' worse than a yellow coward. Well, we'll remember you hiding behind mama's skirts as we go off to fight."

"Aw, lay off. I ain't no slacker," the other man muttered. "And besides, you're too old to join up."

Clancy went on, ignoring Smitty's remark. "And we got a town full of cowards walkin' around here in their fancy hats like they own the place, but they're yellow. They were yellow in the last war and they're gonna' quit on America in the next one too. Them Amish. It sticks in my craw, the way they're always talkin' about loving one another while they let real Americans who love their country die for them, and they don't lift a finger. They're cowards, plain and simple. Ain't nobody more yellow than the Amish, and if I'm wrong, well, say it ain't so."

"It ain't so," said a quiet voice.

. . .

I hadn't noticed when the young man stepped up to the bar just a few feet from the table of drunks, so when the quiet voice corrected Clancy, I looked up. Standing at the bar was a tall, dark-haired man in his early twenties. He had the look of someone who had seen hard work. He had broad shoulders, long arms, a handsome, symmetrical face, and piercing blue eyes.

"Whad'ya say?" asked Clancy, turning to face the newcomer.

"I said the Amish aren't cowards," said the young man.

"Sure they are," said Clancy. "Yellow-bellied stinking traitors who let the real men die while they hide out on their farms and live off the fat of the land."

"They love their country as much as you say you do. Besides, I think you're probably just a lot of talk," said the stranger.

"Whatta ya mean by that?" snarled Clancy.

"I mean that in my short life, I've observed that those that know, don't say, and those that say, don't know. From listening to you spout off, I'd say that despite all your brave talk, the first time a machine gun slug whispers past your ear, you'll cut and run."

"Why you!" shouted Clancy as he rose and pushed his chair back so that it tumbled over behind him. "I'll show you who's gonna cut and run."

Clancy grabbed a beer bottle by its neck from the table and smashed it against the bar. He was stepping forward to thrust his weapon into the young man's face.

That's when I stepped in.

"Lemme go, I'm gonna kill this guy," yelled Clancy, twisting around. I just gave his arm a little squeeze, and the bottle dropped out of his hand.

"Fight fair, Clancy."

My intervention did not deter him. "Aw, lay off, Bobby. I don't need nothing to show pretty boy here how to keep his mouth shut."

I remember shaking my head and admonishing Clancy. "From the looks of the arms on this lad, I would reconsider what you're about to do." Clancy swore at me...

HE LURCHED AT THE STRANGER AND TOOK A WILD SWING. THE MAN slipped out of the way of the haymaker and raised his hands with the palms facing out.

"I don't think you want to do this, mister," the tall young man said quietly.

Clancy roared a profanity and then took another swing, but the stranger ducked beneath it. Quick as a flash, he let Clancy have it with a powerful right hand to the stomach and a stunning left fist to the point of his chin. Clancy stayed upright for a moment, but the light had gone out of his eyes. He swayed forward and fell like a log onto another table, scattering glasses and patrons.

"WELL, THE BARTENDER THREW CLANCY AND HIS BUDDIES OUT OF the bar, and Reuben and I had a few beers and got to know each other. I asked him where an Amish kid learned to throw a left hook like that. He told me he had a Jewish friend that taught him how to box. So, as you have been saying, things are not as they seem. An Amish kid learning to box from a Jew. A week later, he moved into my place, and eight months later we were sailing to Guadalcanal. We were best friends until the day he died."

Bobby looked away for a minute and wiped his eyes with his sleeve. Then he turned back, smiling. "What do you have there?"

Jenny stood up and went to Bobby. She slipped her arms around him and laid her head on his shoulder. "Uncle Bobby, you're just an old softie. I thank God every day that you were Papa's best friend."

Bobby hugged her back, and they stayed that way for a long time. Then Jenny went to the desk and grabbed up her notes.

"Here's where we are."

20

———

THE END OF THE STORY...

Jenny walked slowly down the hall to the Wooster police station interview room. Roberta Kelley had arrived from Pennsylvania three days after Thanksgiving and had given Elbert permission for Jenny to talk with her. Jenny had been anticipating and yet dreading the interview. There were so many things unresolved about this case. Jenny paused at the door and breathed a prayer.

Gott, gib mir Weisheit und hilf mir, diesem Schlamassel auf den Grund zu gehen.

She pushed the door open slowly. Roberta Kelley was sitting at the table in a jailhouse orange jump suit. She was not wearing handcuffs, but there was an officer sitting unobtrusively in the room's corner. Roberta was picking idly at her fingernails. When she heard the click of the latch, she stopped and looked around. When she saw Jenny, she looked away. "The great Jenny Hershberger. Should I be honored?"

Not off to a good start.

Jenny slid into the seat opposite Roberta. Roberta was a forty-ish, peroxide blonde who was attractive in a rough-hewn sort of way. "Thank you for letting me speak with you. I have a few ques-

159

tions I think might help clear up the mystery surrounding Danny Wittmer."

It seemed to Jenny that Roberta paled. She looked down. "I don't know nothing about that."

"Roberta, at some point you are going to have to tell the truth about this." Jenny spread out the papers in her folder in front of Roberta. "These are the sworn affidavits of Perry Miller and three of Levon Wittmer's cousins testifying that you were present with Levon Wittmer and Danny Wittmer in both Colorado and Pennsylvania." She pushed another document forward. "And this is a hotel receipt from Shipshewana, Indiana, showing that you, Levon, and Danny stayed in a hotel room there for three days. During that time, someone murdered Mervin Beier, Danny's grandfather."

Roberta looked up with a jerk. "Murdered, he didn't say nothing..." She realized she had slipped up, and she went silent.

Jenny continued. "Yes, Roberta, murdered. The police have the murder weapon and a clear set of fingerprints that, when Levon arrives, I am sure will prove to be his. Don't you see, Roberta? You must tell what you know. It's the only way you will keep from going to the electric chair or facing lethal injection. It's foolish to keep up this pretense."

"He's coming here? You found him?"

Jenny could see hatred rise in Roberta's face. She played a hunch. "You must hate him very much, Roberta. Otherwise, why would you send me that letter? You set about to destroy Levon, but by signing your own name, you implicated yourself and landed right in the middle of this mess. You're in it all the way, and only if you cooperate with us will there be any hope for leniency."

Roberta's shoulders dropped. She put her face in her hands and wept. "I hate him, I hate him."

"Why Roberta?"

"He told me he loved me, but he never did. He beat me bad

when he was drunk. He cheated on me, he got another girlfriend, then he threw me out."

"Then why don't you just help us?"

Roberta looked at Jenny. "I can't."

"Why not?"

"You don't know him, Jenny. He'll kill me."

Jenny reached across and put her hand on Roberta's. "But he's in custody."

"Doesn't matter. If I rat him out, he'll find a way."

———

ELBERT FINISHED THE REPORTS FROM THE TEXAS SHERIFF'S department and put them on his desk. It was all there. He looked up at Jenny and Bobby. "Let's go talk to this guy."

They walked down the hall and into the interview room. This time, they shackled the prisoner to the chair, and three police officers stood against the walls.

The man in the chair wore a beard, but it did not hide the terrible scarring on the left side of his face. He grinned. "What's this, an Amish Homeward Bound movie?" He chuckled at his little joke, but Elbert did not smile. The three of them sat down across the table from Levon.

Elbert laid his folder down and took out the papers. "First, we have a minor matter of identification to resolve. Somewhat like that old game show. Will the real Levon Wittmer please stand up?"

"What are you talking about, cop? I'm Levon Wittmer."

Elbert shook his head. "Oh, I don't think so. In fact, I know you are not, Eli."

The man's face tightened, and he pulled at his bindings, but he was securely fastened.

"Jenny, would you read the disinterment report from Texas?"

Jenny took the report from Elbert. "We were very curious

about you. From all reports, Levon Wittmer was a kind man, a loving husband, and a good father to Danny. So, when we heard descriptions of the Levon who returned from Texas, it made us wonder. The Texas Levon was the same build as the Pennsylvania Levon, wore the same clothes, had the right ID, and was accompanied by Danny Wittmer, Levon's son. But the behavior was atypical. The Texas Levon was mean, disinterested in his son, and had taken up with a new female companion only a year after the death of his beloved wife. So, we asked the Randall County sheriff for permission to disinter the three bodies that were buried after the fire that you claim killed your friend, Eli Saunders."

The prisoner scowled. "Yeah, he died in the fire. I tried to save him. That's how I got burned."

"We don't believe that's how it happened and now we have the proof," Bobby interjected.

"What proof?"

Elbert nodded. "Jenny?"

Jenny opened the report. "It's a long report, so I'll just read the conclusions. After disinterring the bodies, the Randall County forensics team did a DNA analysis. Two of the bodies were of Hispanic bloodlines, which confirms the story about the cartel members. But the third body, well, that's where your story falls apart."

Levon paled.

"They confirmed the third body to be Levon Wittmer. They matched DNA from his cousins and found a 99% likelihood of relationship, with a common ancestor only two generations away."

Jenny put down the report. "Anything to say?"

"It's baloney! I'm Levon Wittmer."

Elbert nodded to one guard. "Would you bring in Daniel?"

The guard left, and in a minute came back with Daniel King.

Daniel walked up to the table. The prisoner looked up. "Should I know you?"

Daniel smiled, but his eyes were grim. "Since we were best friends growing up, I would think you would."

"Uh... yeah... Daniel. Sure, you were my best friend."

"Really? Then what's my last name?"

"I don't know. I've had trouble with my memory since that fire."

"One question then, and you should remember this, because the answer will tell you my last name as well as how your family business got started. What was the name of the Morgan stallion we sold you and your dad that got your Morgan business established?"

The prisoner looked around. "Uh... stallion? Uh..." The prisoner knit his brows. Then his face brightened. "Figure? Yeah, Figure."

Daniel shook his head. "That's a good guess, but Figure was the founding stallion of the Morgan breed of horses and is the horse to which all Morgans are related. Levon probably told you that. No, the stallion Levon's papa bought from mine was Black King. And that's my last name, King. Daniel King. Do you remember now?"

The prisoner looked up at Daniel and then turned his head away.

"No? I didn't think you would, Eli."

Elbert nodded, and Daniel turned and walked out of the room.

Elbert turned to the man across the table. "We have positive proof you are indeed Eli Saunders. For one thing, your fingerprints. We have a complete set from the Randall County sheriff—from that little marijuana bust you were involved in."

"Ha, I burned my fingers too badly in the fire."

Jenny shook her head. "Because of the engrained imprinting in the deeper skin layers, once exposure to the abrasive, caustic or hot conditions ceases, the fingerprints will grow back. They were already partially regenerated when you killed Mervin Beier. You thought you would get away with that by pulling the tree down on top of the body, but you didn't wipe the hammer. Got two nice clear prints that you left in Mervin's blood."

The prisoner raised his voice. "I'm Levon Wittmer I tell you. How else would I know about the farm and the cousins? How else would I get Danny?"

Jenny took out some more papers. "When you met Levon Wittmer, he was depressed, crushed by the death of his wife. You started plying him with drugs and he started telling you all about his life, his wife, his son, his farm. He forgot to tell you about Daniel, of course."

Elbert continued. "The way Jenny sees it, and I agree, is that you had been selling pot you got from the cartel. You had fifty thousand they were coming to pick up, but you planned to kill the two drug cartel members and take the money. We think you told Levon, and he tried to talk you out of it. Maybe he reminded you the cartel had members all over the world and even had plants in some law enforcement agencies. He told you it wouldn't take long for them to find out there were only two bodies and they would be after you." He looked over at Jenny. "Jenny, want to fill in the rest of the story?"

Jenny took over. "People you both worked with had remarked how closely you and Levon resembled each other, same height and build, same hair color, so you came up with a solution to the problem Levon presented you with. You knew he was right. If there were three bodies in the fire, not just two, it might throw them off your trail long enough for you to take the fifty thousand and hide somewhere. It was easy for you. You killed Levon and swapped clothes. Then when the cartel people came for their money, you killed them. But you didn't count on one of them getting off a shot that hit the propane tank on the back porch. The house went up like a torch and you couldn't get the money. It got burned up in the fire. I believe that's how you got burned—not trying to save someone... but trying to get the money. That's why you went through the charade with Danny. You figured you would take him to Smicksburg as proof of who you were and sell the farm. Then you'd have plenty of money."

Eli Saunders snarled. "You're pretty smart for a woman."

Jenny smiled. "Being a woman has nothing to do with it. Once I understood what 'things are not what they seem' meant, everything fell into place. A Levon that was not Levon. That was the only answer. We confirmed that with the fingerprints on the hammer compared with yours. The DNA from Texas and Daniel's identification are just the icing on the cake."

Elbert stood. "Eli Saunders, I am arresting you for the murders of Levon Wittmer, Jerry and Sarah Miller, Mervin Beier, and Danny Wittmer."

Saunders laughed. "Like I said, you're pretty smart. But you got it wrong about Levon. He was too stoned to figure out about counting the bodies. I figured that before Levon even came over that night. So, when he walked in the door... boom, three bodies."

"Get him out of here," Elbert said.

The guards came and unshackled the prisoner. Saunders stood up and turned to go, and then he turned back to Jenny. "You may get me on the first four, but I didn't have nothing to do with the kid's death. You need to ask someone else about that."

Jenny frowned. "What do you mean?"

"You better ask her."

"Her?"

"Yeah, Bobbie Kelley. She was the last one to see Danny Wittmer alive. She's the one who got him from the nut house."

"The nut house? What are you talking about?"

"Not so smart after all, are ya? The nut house right here in town. Danny Wittmer was right in your backyard for a year and you never knew it."

21

DANNY

Jenny stared after Eli Saunders as the guards led him out. He was still laughing.

Eldon looked at Jenny. "What did he mean, Danny was in our backyard for a year?"

Bobby answered. "The only place Saunders can be talking about is the Apple Creek Developmental Center in Apple Creek."

The light came on in Jenny's head. "Yes, I know it well. It's only about three blocks from my old house. When we were kids, we used to call it the Cuckoo's Nest. It wasn't very nice, but kids are a little insensitive sometimes. Someone like Danny could easily have been placed there. And that would explain where he was for an entire year. Elbert, I need to talk to Roberta, if that's all right."

Elbert nodded yes. "That's fine. You can probably get more out of her than I can."

Jenny looked up as Roberta came into the room. She pointed to the chair opposite her and Roberta sat down.

"Is he here? Did you say I said anything, 'cause I didn't."

Jenny shook her head. "No, you said nothing, but he did."

Roberta's mouth flew open. "What did he say?"

"He said you were the last one to see Danny alive. That you were the one who got Danny out of the Apple Creek Developmental Center, just about the time they found Danny murdered. We called the center. They confirmed Danny was there, and that someone came and got him, but they weren't sure who. We have the name of the doctor that signed the commitment papers. Dr. McIntyre. He was in Smicksburg. When we called him, he also confirmed that a Levon Wittmer had Danny committed. So, we are questioning any staff that was there at the time. You could not have removed Danny unless you had Levon's signed approval, or you knew someone on the staff. Believe me, we will find out, so you might as well tell us."

Roberta almost choked. "I.. I.."

"Look, Roberta. We know this man is not Levon Wittmer. He is a murderer named Eli Saunders. You've been protecting him, but I know you really want to see him in prison... or dead. Otherwise, you would not have started all this with the letter. Please Roberta, for Danny's sake, tell us the truth. Don't be afraid. We'll protect you."

Roberta looked around like she wanted to run, but the deputy was watching. She looked down at the table. "He was going to kill Danny."

"What?"

"Eli was going to kill Danny and I couldn't let that happen. I really liked Danny."

"Why do you say that?"

"When Levon... when Eli sold the farm, he had a couple hundred thousand dollars. He didn't need Danny anymore, so he got that doctor to commit him. But he didn't pay the bills, so the hospital contacted Eli and told him to pay up or come get Danny.

Eli figured he'd just go get Danny, kill him, and disappear. No more worries. I decided I had to do something."

Jenny put her hand on Roberta's. "How did you get involved in all this, dear?"

"I met Eli in Texas. I was working in a bar and he was a real high roller. Always had money and pot to smoke. Then he started bringing this Levon guy around. I felt sorry for the kid. His wife had died, his son was messed up, and he was awfully depressed. Eli got him high and Levon could forget about everything."

"Then the whole incident with the drug cartel shootout happened?"

"Yeah. When he killed those guys in Texas, he thought he was going to have fifty thousand. But he figured if there were only two bodies, the cartel would come after him. So, he killed Levon, swapped clothes with him and burned the house down around them. But the money burned up, and so did his face."

"So he needed another way to get some money?"

Roberta nodded. "Yeah, he knew about Levon's farm, so he figured out that he could go get Danny to prove he was Levon and sell the farm to the cousins. After he got out of the hospital, he went to Levon's place and got all his stuff—birth certificate, information about Danny, you know, all his papers."

"Yes, but he didn't have Eliza's birth certificate, so he had to go to Shipshewana after he got Danny."

"Right, but the Millers suspected something was fishy and Eli caught on to them. After he got Danny, he waited for them to leave the place and he pulled them over. He made them drive to Wheeler Mountain, and he killed them there. He made me follow and pick him up after he dumped the car."

"So, you knew he killed the Millers?"

"Yes, but I didn't know he killed the grandfather. He left me at the hotel and drove out to see the Beiers with Danny."

"And Mervin suspected it wasn't Levon?"

"He must have. Eli brought Danny back with the things he got from them and he was all worked up. Kept talkin' about the old man being a wise guy. The next day, he left us at the hotel all day. When he came back he was relaxed, easy. Never talked about old man Beier again. We stayed one more night and headed for Pennsylvania."

"And you were driving Levon's truck?"

"Yes. We got to Pennsylvania, we spent as little time as we could with Levon's cousins and sold the farm. We had to wait around until Escrow closed. That's when Eli took Danny to Apple Creek and committed him."

Jenny had been making notes. She looked up. "So, Danny was there for a year and then they called Eli about unpaid bills?"

"Yeah, he owed them ten thousand. Eli thought he might need Danny again for something, but when he found out how much it cost to keep him there, he told me he was going to go get Danny and kill him. Danny was a good kid for all his troubles. Eli went on a drunk and beat me up real bad. It was the last straw. I took a lot of Eli's money and I took the truck. I went to get Danny. I was going to take him back to his grandparents. When they asked me for papers from Danny's father, I offered one of the attendants a grand to get Danny for me. I went back that night and she brought Danny out. I took off for Indiana, but it was snowing, snowing so hard."

"What happened then, Roberta?"

"We got stuck in the snow. It was coming down so hard I couldn't see and I drove off the road. The kid had been crying all the way from Apple Creek. I tried to shut him up. I was scared. I was sure Eli was right on my tail, that he knew I was going to Shipshewana to tell the Beiers. When I got out to look at the car, Danny slipped out of the back seat with his horse and his book and took off."

"You followed him to the shed?"

"Yes, he was inside. He was screaming, screaming so much. I was so scared Eli would find us and kill us both. I tried to make him stop. I... I put my hand over his mouth, but he wouldn't stop. I pressed down hard, but he wouldn't stop... and then..."

"What happened then, Roberta?"

"He... he went limp. It was like he went to sleep, but I couldn't wake him up. I tried. I tried to blow air into his lungs, but he was... he was..." Roberta put her face into her hands and wept.

Jenny came around the table and put her arm around Roberta. "He was dead?"

"Yes... yes... He was dead. I couldn't just leave him there in a heap, so I did him up as best as I could. You know, like at a funeral home."

Jenny nodded. "You really cared for Danny, didn't you?"

"The poor kid didn't have no one. He didn't have no mother, no dad... I wanted to save him from Eli, but I killed him instead. I didn't mean to. He wouldn't stop screaming and I was so afraid of Eli..."

Jenny knelt beside Roberta and let her sob.

Bobby nodded as Jenny finished telling him and Elbert about her conversation with Roberta. Jenny sighed. "So now we know how it happened. It wasn't Eli, it was Roberta. What will happen to her, Elbert?"

Elbert shook his head. "Well, if the jury believes her story, and they just might, she won't be charged with murder in Danny's death. Probably involuntary manslaughter. But she was an accessory to all of Eli's crimes, so whatever happens with Danny's case, and even if she testifies against Eli, Roberta will be in prison a long, long time."

"And Eli?"

"There isn't a jury in the world that won't send him to death row. We have solid proof he killed Mervin Beier, and if Roberta will testify, we can pin the Miller's deaths and Levon Wittmer's death on him. I think she's at that place now. Eli Saunders is finished."

"So, what's left to tie all this up?"

Jenny looked at Bobby. "I think we should see about getting Levon and Danny's remains so we can bury them with Eliza in Pennsylvania. How does that work, Elbert?"

Elbert scratched his head. "Well, we have to make a disinterment and transfer request. The highest level of authority is a representative directed by the deceased individual to carry out his/her will. Since there is no will, following that, in order, is a spouse, child, parent, or sibling. If these avenues are exhausted, the degree of kinship, that is the closest living relative, will determine disinterment authority. In this case, since Eliza and Levon are both deceased and Levon's parents are also deceased, and there is no will, then Amanda Beier will have to sign the request."

"So, one more trip to Shipshewana?"

"Looks like it."

Jenny and Bobby were back in Apple Creek. They had gotten the disinterment and transfer order with Amanda's help, and Jenny was sitting in the front room thinking about the entire series of events. It was a bitter December day and a bright fire was burning in the fireplace. As she gazed into the coals, the familiar thought came to her. "Things are not as they seem, Jenny."

What?

"Things are not as they seem."

What does that mean, Lord? We solved the case. Danny's going home, Levon's going home, it's all wrapped up.

"Things are not as they seem, Jenny."

And then it came to her. She gasped at the thought. Then quickly she got up and went into the kitchen where Bobby and

Daniel were playing checkers. "Bobby, I need to call Elbert right away."

Bobby reached into his pocket and handed Jenny his phone.

Jenny took it and dialed Elbert's number.

"Elbert Wainwright."

"Elbert, this is Jenny. I had a thought, and I wonder if we could do one more thing before we close this case."

"Sure, Jenny, your hunches have been spot on so far."

"Well, I was just wondering if..."

<hr>

THREE DAYS LATER, BOBBY GOT THE CALL FROM ELBERT. THEY WERE all gathered in the kitchen for dinner.

"This is Bobby. Oh, hi, Elbert. What's up?" "Yeah, I know Jenny asked you to request that." There was a pause. "What! You're kidding! No, I'll tell her. Boy, this sure throws a monkey wrench in the works. Thanks."

Bobby closed the phone and looked at Jenny. "They ran the DNA test on the remains of Danny Wittmer that they removed from the grave in Indiana."

Jenny felt an excitement grow. "And..."

"The Boy In Blue Denim is not Danny Wittmer."

Everyone stared at Jenny. She smiled. "It's all right. I think I know the answer to this puzzle."

22

LIFE FROM THE DEAD

Jenny Hershberger waited in the office at the Apple Creek Development Center. The administrator listened to her story and then got on the intercom and paged a staff member. In a few minutes, the intercom clicked.

"This is Bernice."

The administrator, Charlene Bergman, answered. "Bernice, I need to see you in my office."

"Well, I'm in the middle of something. Can I come when I'm finished?"

"Actually, Bernice, no. I need you in my office right now."

"Okay. Be right there." The intercom clicked. In a minute, there was a knock on the door.

"Come in."

The door opened partway and an older woman with graying hair looked in.

"Come in, Bernice, and sit down."

The woman paled and came in hesitantly. "Did I do something wrong?"

"That remains to be seen. Come in."

Bernice came all the way into the room and then sat in the

chair Charlene pointed to. She sat on the edge of the chair and clasped her hands together.

"Bernice, this is Jenny Hershberger. She has a few questions for you."

"How can I help you, Ms. Hershberger?"

Jenny pulled out her notebook and turned to a page further back in the book. "Bernice, I am attached to the Wooster police department as a special investigator. I am going to ask you some direct questions. We already know part of the answer, so it would be best for you and for the case I am working on if you just answer truthfully and without evasion."

"Do I need a lawyer?"

"No, I am not arresting you, nor are you being charged with anything. I just need some honest answers."

Bernice looked frightened. "I'll... I'll do my best."

Jenny smiled. "Good. Now let's get right to it. Do you know a woman named Roberta Kelley?"

Bernice looked at her boss. She was wringing her hands now.

Charlene spoke. "Answer the question please, Bernice."

Bernice slumped down. "Yes," she answered quietly.

Jenny asked another question. "Did you ever have dealings with her concerning one of your patients, a ten-year-old boy named Danny Wittmer?"

Bernice nodded. "Yes."

"Can you tell me about that, please?"

Bernice sighed and pushed back in her chair. "I'm going to lose my job, aren't I?"

Charlene looked at Bernice. "You may, but I think the statute of limitations for what I think you did has run out, so I'm not sure you can get in trouble there. That said, you might as well get it off your chest."

"Okay, I'll tell you. Yes, Roberta Kelley came in to see about taking Danny home from the Center."

"And when was this?" asked Jenny.

"In the winter of 1995. She was terribly upset. I told her she needed to have official permission, either from a doctor or a parent. She told me she didn't have that, but that it was a matter of life and death, that Danny's life was in danger. If I wanted to see Danny stay alive, I needed to help. She sounded like she meant it."

Jenny pressed on. "And then what happened?"

"She... she offered me money. A thousand dollars. It was more money than I made in a month. And she really was telling the truth. I could see it in her eyes. So, I told her to come back that night, late, and I would bring her Danny."

"And did you?"

Bernice nodded. "Yes. I went down to Danny's room about 3 a.m. He was sound asleep, so I got him up, got him dressed, got his things, you know, his horse and his book, and took him out the back. Roberta was waiting for me. I handed Danny over. She gave me the money, and that was that. I never heard from her or Danny again."

"And you signed the papers releasing Danny, and Roberta forged Levon Wittmer's signature?"

Bernice nodded.

Jenny leaned forward. "Did you know they found a young boy that was later identified as Danny Wittmer dead in the snow in Indiana the next day? Someone had suffocated him. Roberta Kelley has confessed to the crime."

Bernice started to get up, her face pale, and a few random beads of sweat breaking out on her brow.

"Sit down, Bernice," Charlene said softly.

Bernice sank back into her chair.

Jenny proceeded. "You knew that, didn't you? You saw the story of The Boy In Blue Denim in the paper and you knew it was Danny, but you told nobody because of your part in it. You knew the dead boy was Danny ten years ago. You could have gone to the police and cleared the mystery up."

Tears came into Bernice's eyes. "Yes, I saw the story in the newspaper. I didn't know what to do. If I told anyone, they would have put me in jail. I was a single mother with kids. They would have taken my children away." Bernice burst into tears.

Jenny sighed. "Now, I want to tell you the rest of the story, Bernice. After ten years in a grave marked Johnny Doe, The Boy In Blue Denim, we thought we identified the boy as Danny Wittmer. However, when we disinterred the body for shipment back to Pennsylvania, we had the DNA of the remains checked by the LaGrange County coroner. The remains were not Danny Wittmer's. We do not know who the boy is."

Bernice straightened up and her eyes bugged out. "What?"

"The remains were not Danny Wittmer's."

Bernice paled, and then a look of horror came over her face. "Oh dear God! Jimmy!"

"Who?"

"Jimmy Weston."

"Who's Jimmy Weston?"

"He was Danny's best friend. We used to call them The Bobbsey Twins. They looked so much alike, both blonde, both were autistic. They could have been brothers. Jimmy was the only one that Danny could relate to."

"Did they sleep in the same room?"

"Yes, they were roommates. I... I must have sent Jimmy!"

"What?"

"I must have sent Jimmy with Roberta Kelley. I told you it was very late. I was tired. I went in the room and thought I woke up Danny. He was groggy. I made him put on Danny's clothes and took him. He didn't say a word. Danny must have been hiding under his covers."

"And later you couldn't tell you had made a mistake?"

Bernice shook her head. "When I saw the picture of The Boy In Blue Denim in the newspaper, I was scared. I really thought it was Danny. He had Danny's clothes on. And like I said, they could have been twins..."

Jenny looked at Charlene. "And you knew nothing?"

Charlene shook her head. "I've only been here four years. They told me the boy that is here is Jimmy Weston and all his records are in order... I didn't even know about Danny Wittmer."

Jenny asked the question that had been on her heart for four days. "Does the person you call Jimmy Weston still live here?"

Charlene nodded. "Jimmy is a ward of the state. He has no known family. He'll be here until he dies, or the place closes. He hasn't said a word for years. It's like he's catatonic."

"Can I see him, please?"

Jenny walked into the sitting room. A few of the inmates of the Center were sitting around quietly. Charlene pointed to a young man in the corner who was sitting by the window looking out. He was about twenty, with blond longish hair, very hand-some. Charlene took Jenny over.

"Jimmy, this is Jenny."

The young man looked up at the little Amish woman standing there. "You look like my mama."

Charlene's mouth opened in surprise. "He spoke!"

"May I sit down?" Jenny asked.

The young man nodded.

"I have something for you."

The young man looked up. Jenny reached into her bag and brought out the reader. The young man's eyes opened wide. Then Jenny reached in again and brought out the rainbow horse.

The young man smiled, a big smile. "Horse!"

Jenny nodded. "Yes, Danny, it is Horse."

The young man took the stuffed horse and set it on the table next to his chair. "Time for school, Horse." He began speaking in a soft voice.

"Run, Tom, said Mother. Run, Betty, run. It is time for school. Run fast!"

The young man's eyes closed as he continued speaking to Horse.

"Away ran Tom and Betty. Goodbye, Mother, they called.

"We are on our way to school. Goodbye, Flip.

"Flip saw Tom and Betty go. He wanted to go to school, too. He wanted to run after Tom. But he did not go…"

Danny Wittmer kept speaking to Horse, His face was aglow and a huge smile wreathed it.

Jenny's heart filled.

Thank you, Lord. You have brought me full circle. You rescued me from a storm and now You have rescued Danny. He was lost and now he is found. Danke, du lieber Gott.

Things are not always what they seem, Jenny…

Jenny sat with Rachel in the back seat of the van. They were going home to Paradise. Rachel leaned against her mama.

"So how did Roberta know about the Quilt Fair?"

"Roberta Kelley was very interested in the Amish. When she lived in Centerville, she read my column every week. She found out about my books, so she bought them all. She particularly loved *A Quilt For Jenna.* So, when she wanted to get my attention, she mentioned the Dalton Quilt Fair. She knew that would draw me in."

Rachel smiled. "Well, that certainly worked. But why did she hate Eli so much?"

Jenny sighed. "Roberta was a gullible girl. When she fell in love with Eli in Texas, she was young and impressionable. He always had money and drugs and she just got in over her head. He got her hooked and then used her addiction to the drugs to control her. So, she helped him when he killed the Millers. And after that, she took care of Danny until Eli put him in the Apple Creek Center. In her own way, she really cared for Danny. She and Eli lived in Centerville for a while, at the house we went to. Remember the old man in Centerville who said the boyfriend who lived with Bobbie was mean? Well, Eli beat her up, especially when he was drunk. Roberta was one of those abused women who just can't leave. Then, after a while, Eli tired of her, got another woman, and threw her out. That's when she snapped. She knew he was going to kill Danny, so she got there first. If she had not gone, Danny would really be dead now. As it was, Jimmy Weston was an innocent victim."

Rachel shook her head. "And after she thought she had killed Danny, she blamed Eli for everything bad that happened to her."

Jenny looked at Rachel. "Yes. All these years, she wrestled with her guilt and her hate. She became obsessed with getting revenge, and she knew she could do that by implicating Eli in the murders. So, when she saw the story about The Boy In Blue Denim in the local newspaper, she wrote the letter to me. She knew about the case we had solved, the Emma Johnson case, and she knew if she hooked me in with the references to my own story, she might bring Eli to judgement. I don't think she realized we would find her, too."

"And then the Lord spoke to you through those old pictures. He let you know that there were things about this case that were not as they seemed."

Jenny nodded. "Two Levons and two Dannys. A real puzzle. But what I've found from living in a small town like Paradise is people who commit crimes usually give themselves away. Eli couldn't carry off pretending to be Levon, even though Levon had told him just about everything concerning his life. He didn't fool the Millers, and he didn't fool Mervin Beier."

"What will happen to Danny, Mama?"

"When Bernice took Horse and Danny's book and sent them with Jimmy, she took away his last connection to reality. He retreated inside himself and stayed there for ten years. He's already made a remarkable improvement. It's like he's come back from the dead."

Rachel snuggled closer to Jenny. "He did, Mama, thanks to you."

"Danny is going to move to an autism center in Greenfield, Indiana. Jane Thompson and Granny Eckert have volunteered to take Amanda to visit her grandson, often. Who knows? With the Lord's help and genuine love from Amanda, maybe Danny can go live with her in time."

"And it will certainly help to bring Amanda back to life to know that at least one of her loved ones is still alive."

"Yes. When Granny and Jane went to tell her, Jane said she cried and cried. Then she told Granny she needed to get herself together so she could go see Danny as soon as he moved in, and help him as much as she could."

"Oh, Mama. You solved another mystery."

Jenny looked out the window at the Pennsylvania countryside flashing by. "You know, Granny Eckert said something to me that I'm just now understanding."

"What's that, Mama?"

"She said to me, 'God works in mysterious ways. If Jenna had not died, you would not be here today, Jenny.'"

Rachel thought for a moment. "So, if Jenna had not died, *Grossmütter* Jerusha would not have decided to leave the church. She would not have made the quilt for Jenna and she would not have gone to the Dalton Quilt Fair."

Jenny nodded. "And I would have frozen to death in the back of that car at Jepson's Pond because my mama would not have found me."

"And then you would not have been alive to find Danny. Oh my."

Jenny put her arms around Rachel and pulled her very close. "And I would not have had you, my blessed *tochter*."

Rachel smiled and shook her head. "So, Danny Wittmer was right there in Apple Creek all these years. Amazing." Then she patted her mama's hand. *"Und wir wissen, dass denen, die Gott lieben, alle Dinge zum Guten dienen, denen, die nach seinem Vorsatz berufen sind."*

"Yes, Rachel, all things work together for good..."

"What are you two talking about back there?" Bobby asked.

Rachel squeezed her mama. "Oh, we were just reminding ourselves how kind and gracious the Lord is."

Jenny only smiled.

ABOUT THE AUTHOR

Patrick E. Craig is an award-winning author with eighteen published novels. He has won three CIBA Book Awards, a Selah Award and a Word Guild Book Award. His work includes six Amish novels, three World War II historical novels with a short story sequel, two anthologies of Amish stories, a standalone novel and a memoir, and two YA paranormal books. He lives in Idaho with his wife Judy.

MORE BOOKS BY PATRICK E.CRAIG

The Quilt That Knew

A Quilt For Jenna

The Road Home

Jenny's Choice

The Amish Heiress

The Amish Princess

The Mennonite Queen

The Journals of Jenny Hershberger

The Amish Menorah and Other Stories

A Christmas Collection

The Gettysburg Letter

Far On The Ringing Plains

The Scepter And The Isle

Men Who Strove With Gods

Beyond The Red Hills

The Drive

Say Goodbye To The River

The Mystery of Ghost Dancer Ranch

The Lost Coast

Contact Patrick at pec@patrickecraig.com

Website: https://www.patrickecraig.com

Find These Books at Patrick's Amazon Page :

https://tinyurl.com/y3nwsmgs

THE APPLE CREEK DREAMS SERIES

Book 1—A Quilt For Jenna

Jerusha Springer has spent months making the most beautiful quilt anyone in Apple Creek, Ohio has ever seen, and she knows it is going to take first prize at the Quilt Fair in Dalton. The prize money will be her ticket out of the Amish way of life—away from the memories of Jenna, the daughter she lost a year ago and Reuben, her tormented husband, who has been missing since Jenna's death.

On the way to the fair, Jerusha gets caught in the Storm of The Century. An accident leaves her trapped in her driver's car—and trapped by the memories of her marriage to Reuben and the loss of little Jenna. And then another littler girl enters the story and takes Jerusha's heart captive in a way she hadn't expected. Can this child also be the one to heal Reuben's pain as well?

A beautiful story of loss and redemption.

Book 2—The Road Home

Author Patrick Craig continues the story of Jenny Springer, the child rescued in A Quilt for Jenna, with a story of reconciliation and healing.

Jenny Springer is the local historian for the Amish community in Apple Creek, Ohio. When Jenny was a child, Jerusha Hershberger Springer rescued her from a terrible snowstorm, and when no trace of Jenny's parents could be found, the Springer family adopted her. Since then, the burning desire in Jenny's heart is to find out who she really is.

Then Jenny meets Jonathan Hershberger, a drifter from San Francisco who lands in Apple Creek fleeing a drug deal gone wrong. Intrigued by an *Englischer* with an Amish name, Jenny offers to help him discover his Amish roots. When together they dig into Jonathan's past, Jenny gets serious in her own search for her long-lost parents. And as they travel The Road Home together, Jenny finds the truly surprising answer to her deepest questions, while Jonathan discovers his need for a home, a family, and a relationship with God.

Book 3—Jenny's Choice

Jonathan and Jenny Hershberger are happily settled in Paradise, Pennsylvania on the farm Jenny inherited from her grandfather. But when Jonathan disappears in a terrible boating accident, Jenny and her young daughter, Rachel, return home to Apple Creek, Ohio to live with her adoptive parents, Reuben and Jerusha Springer.

As Jenny works through her grief and despair, she discovers she has a gift for writing. A handsome young publisher discovers her work and, after the publication of her first book, Jenny is on the verge of worldly success and possible romance.

Then a conflict arises with the elders of her church, and Jenny must ask herself if she's willing to go outside her faith to pursue her dreams. At the same time, the budding romance is at odds with Jenny's hope that Jonathan might someday be found alive. Jenny must choose and Jenny's Choice leads her to the surprising and heart-warming conclusion of the Apple Creek Dreams series.

THE PARADISE CHRONICLES SERIES

Book 1—The Amish Heiress

Rachel Hershberger's life in Paradise, Pennsylvania is far from happy. Her papa struggles with a terrible event from the past, and his emotional instability has created an irreparable breach between them. Rachel's one desire is to leave the Amish way of life and Paradise forever. Then her prayers are answered. Rachel discovers that the strange, key-shaped birthmark above her heart identifies her as the heiress to a vast fortune left by her *Englischer* grandfather, Robert St. Clair. If Rachel will marry a suitable descendent of the St. Clair family, she will inherit an enormous sum of money. But Rachel does not know that behind the scenes is her long-dead grandfather's sister-in-law, Augusta St. Clair, a vicious woman who will do anything to keep the fortune in her own hands. As the deceptions and intrigues of the St. Clair family bind her in their web, Rachel realizes that she has made a terrible mistake. But has her change of heart come too late?

Book 2—The Amish Princess

Opahtuhwe, the White Deer, is the beautiful daughter of Wingenund, the powerful chief of the Delaware tribe, and a true princess. Everything in her life changes when the renegade known as Scar brings three Amish prisoners to the Delaware camp. Jonathan and Joshua Hershberger are twin brothers that Scar has determined to adopt and teach the Indian way. The third prisoner is Jonas Hershberger, their father, who has been made a slave because he would not defend his family. White Deer is drawn to Jonathan but his hatred of the Indians makes him push her away. Joshua's gentle heart and steadfast refusal to abandon the Amish faith lead White Deer to a life-changing decision, and rejection by her people. In the end, White Deer must choose between the ways of her people and her new-found faith. And complicating it all is her love for the man who can only hate her.

Book 3—The Mennonite Queen

CHANTICLEER INTERNATIONAL BOOK AWARDS SEMI-FINALIST - THE CHAUCER HISTORICAL DIVISION: This is the third book in The Paradise Chronicles series. Isabella, Princess of Poland, is raised to a life of great wealth and leisure in the Polish Royal Court, destined to marry a king. But fate or divine providence intervenes when she meets Johan Hirschberg, a young Anabaptist who works in her father's stable. This chance meeting leads the young couple into a forbidden love. Together they flee Poland and embark on a dangerous journey that brings them, after great peril, to the small parish of a troubled priest named Menno Simons. Catholic Bishop, Franz von Waldek, paid by King Sigismund, Isabella's father to find the princess at all costs, pursues them across Europe. Isabella does not know it, but if von Waldek captures her, she will have to make a choice that will change the course of European history forever.

THE ISLANDS SERIES WITH MURRAY PURA

Book 1—Far On The Ringing Plains

CHANTICLEER INTERNATIONAL BOOK AWARDS FIRST PLACE WINNER — HEMINGWAY 20TH CENTURY WARTIME FICTION.

Far On The Ringing Plains INSPIRED BY TRUE EVENTS In the spirit of The Thin Red Line, Hacksaw Ridge, Flags of our Fathers and Pearl Harbor. Realistic. Gritty. Gutsy. Without taking it too far, Craig and Pura take it far enough to bring war home to your heart, mind, and soul. The rough edge of combat is here. And the rough edge of language, human passion, and our flawed humanity. If you can handle the ruggedness and honesty of Saving Private Ryan, 1917 or Dunkirk, you can handle the power and authenticity of ISLANDS: Far on the Ringing Plains. For the beauty and the honor is here too. Just like the Bible, in all its roughness and realism and truthfulness about life, reaching out for God is ever-present in ISLANDS. So are hope and faith and self-sacrifice. Prayer. Christ. Courage. An indomitable spirit. And the best of human nature, triumphing over the worst. Bud Parmalee, Johnny Strange, Billy Martens—three men that had each other's backs and the backs of every Marine in their company and platoon. All three were raised never to fight. All three saw no other choice but to enlist and try to make a difference. All three would never be the same again. Never. And neither would their world. This is their story.

Book 2—The Scepter and The Isle

CHANTICLEER INTERNATIONAL BOOK AWARDS FINALIST — HEMINGWAY 20TH CENTURY WARTIME FICTION

It did not end with Guadalcanal. It did not end with one island. There were more islands... an island with snow-capped peaks, friendly people, blue seas, where Bud found love with his Tongan princess. Where Billy breathed the clean air of mountains where no danger lurked. Where

Johnny found a way to drain the hate that drove him mad. They found
life again after the death-filled frenzy of Guadalcanal But the God of
war was not done with them. More islands sent their siren call from
beyond distant horizons and they were cast upon dark shores. Islands
with coconut palms, dense green jungle and death. Islands that took
more life than they ever gave back. Islands where women killed like
men, islands filled with the most brutal soldiers the Japanese Empire
could offer. Tarawa. Saipan. Islands that had to be endured. Islands they
had to survive. There was no other way to bring the war to an end.
There was no other way to get home again.

Book 3—Men Who Stove With Gods

**CHANTICLEER INTERNATIONAL BOOK AWARDS FINALIST —
HEMINGWAY 20TH CENTURY WARTIME FICTION** Since 1941 the
Marines have fought the Japanese. They met them first on Guadalcanal,
a maelstrom of death and fury. Tarawa, Saipan, Okinawa—their friends
died beside them, their youth disappeared in a baptism of fire, but they
kept on. Johnny, Bud, and Billy went ashore on bloodstained Okinawa
hungry for the end of the war. But they knew when the battle ended,
they would face their Armageddon on the sacred beaches of Japan.

PRAISE FOR PATRICK E. CRAIG'S BOOKS

"From the first page of *Jenny's Choice* I felt a tender compassion for Jenny, the young woman in this novel. Her story unfolds with a gentle hand and a lyrical tone that leads to an ending filled with hope. As with the other books in the Apple Creek Dreams series, you'll want to read this book in one sitting. Preferably with a cup of tea."

— Robin Jones Gunn, bestselling author of the Glenbrooke series and the Christy Miller series

"Patrick Craig's Apple Creek Dreams series is both poetic and sincere. Strong characters who deal with the grief and joy of everyday life make these stories you'll remember long after you reach the last page....*Jenny's Choice* is a tender story of grief, restoration, and grace."

— Vannetta Chapman, author of the Pebble Creek Series

Patrick Craig writes with an enthusiasm and a passion that is a joy to read. He deals with romance, faith, love, loss, tragedy, and restoration with equal amounts of elegance, grace, clarity, and power. Everyone should pick up *A Quilt For Jenna*, his debut novel in Amish fiction, turn off the phone and computer and TV, and settle in for a good night's read. Craig's book is a blessing.